ANDROVIA

ANDRUVIA

Cameron Cowburn

To order additional copies of this book, contact:
Xlibris
844-714-8691
www.Xlibris.com
Orders@Xlibris.com
822668

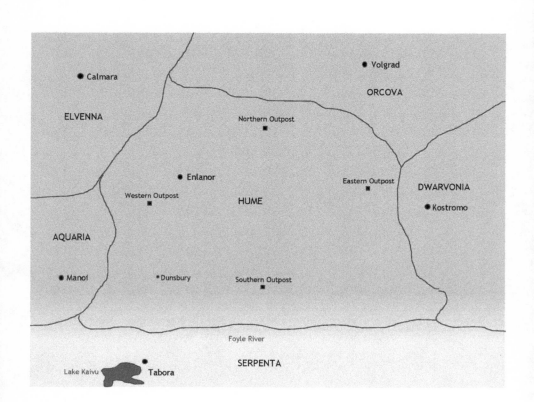

Calmara

ELVENNA

Volgrad

ORCOVA

Northern Outpost

Enlanor

Western Outpost

HUME

Eastern Outpost

DWARVONIA

Kostromo

AQUARIA

Manoi

Dunsbury

Southern Outpost

Foyle River

SERPENTA

Lake Kaivu   Tabora

1

I CAN'T BELIEVE HOW *hot it is today. My armor could probably fry an egg!* thought Finnian as he halted his horse. The bright yellow sun had been beating down upon him and the rest of his platoon all day, and he was certain he wasn't the only one who was silently suffering in the heat. It was one of the hottest summers he could remember, and his platoon's patrol of the northeast sector was turning out to be quite punishing. Finnian almost wished he wasn't wearing armor at all, for the added protection may not have been worth the feeling like you were being cooked in a stone oven.

Finnian was a tall, athletic man of twenty-six years. He had wavy, shoulder-length dark brown hair with bright blue eyes that had always received compliments when he was a young boy. He carried a vertical scar on his left eyebrow—an injury he sustained four years ago during a battle with an Orcovan raiding party. It was perhaps one of the most defining features of his entire face. Though some may have felt self-conscious about it, Finnian rather liked it. For him, it served as a constant reminder to always remain vigilant about the dangers that awaited him in his profession as a soldier.

Finnian was raised in Galwin, a modest-sized community in the northern region of the province of Hume by his parents, Quinn and Caitlin. Because of the community's small size, Finnian didn't have many friends his age growing up, and he was an only child. Instead, he spent his days idolizing his father and challenging him to sparring matches with a wooden training sword he'd gifted to Finnian on his fifth birthday. Though he had long ago graduated to a steel sword, Finnian still had his wooden training sword hanging above his bunk at the barracks to remember his father by.

Quinn was killed during a small skirmish fighting the Orcovans when Finnian was just eight years old, and he had never been the same since. He had always wanted to be a career soldier like his father, and Quinn's death only fueled this desire . . . much to his mother's disappointment.

Six years after his father's death, his mother was killed when the Orcovans raided their village. Finnian only survived by hiding in the woodshed behind their home, and he had always felt a sense of guilt for not being able to protect his mother. Realistically, there was nothing an unarmed fourteen-year-old boy could have done against battle-hardened, highly trained Orcovan warriors, but nothing could convince him otherwise.

After the death of his mother, Finnian lived on his own for a year, which he has always felt was the longest year of his life. He had to be fifteen to be eligible to start his official military training in the Human army, and he had wanted nothing more than to be out on the battlefield clashing arms with the "Orcs," as many in Hume call the people from Orcova. He thought being a Human soldier was the only fitting profession for a boy whose parents were both killed by the loathsome, brutish Orcs.

All males in Hume start their military training at the academy at the age of fifteen and undergo intense training for five years. Every graduate is required to actively serve in the Human army for five years when turning twenty, although many will continue to actively serve after their five years are completed. If a soldier should choose to retire from an active duty status, he will be placed in reserve status and can be called upon at a moment's notice to report for duty should the need arise. However, the Human army was large in number and quite formidable, and the need to be called into active duty rarely ever occurred.

Finnian had a gift for being a soldier. Part of the credit must be given to his father, who made it a point to train Finnian whenever time allowed it, but Finnian also had an inherent fighting ability that simply couldn't be taught. His instincts and ability to adapt in battle made him a natural leader, and his strength, resilience, and athleticism gave him a great aptitude for combat. Finnian's potential was identified not long after entering the academy and was put on a watch list for special units of military service for those who showed promise.

After graduating from the academy, he was selected to be a royal guard at the age of only twenty-one—the youngest man to ever be selected for such a prestigious position. The royal guards were a regiment of approximately two thousand elite soldiers tasked with protecting and escorting the royal family. It was this very position that gifted him with his defining scar over his left eyebrow.

Finnian reached up and ran his gloved fingers across the scar. He remembered the incident well . . .

~

His battalion had been tasked with escorting King Aidan, Queen Evelyn, and their two children, Prince Owen and Princess Reagan. The royal family was traveling to Calmara, the capital of the province of Elvenna.

Elvenna lies along the northwestern border of Hume, and it is home to the Elves. The Elves had held a steady alliance with the Humans for many years, and King Aidan made it a priority to maintain that relationship. The wife of Amrynn, the Elven king, had just given birth to triplet boys. Though the boys were not Amrynn's firstborn children, Aidan wanted to personally congratulate the family and celebrate the extraordinary occurrence. Such celebrations are customary in Andruvia, and they often lasted for days.

The Human royal family set out in their carriage, protected by an entire battalion, early in the morning to ensure they reached Elvenna before sunset. Elvenna and Hume both share a border with Orcova to the northeast, and being so close to the Orcovan border was nerve-wracking enough. Neither the royal family nor their guards relished the thought of being anywhere near the Orcs' border when visibility is low during the night, so they made haste to beat the fall of darkness.

The trip had been quiet and uneventful all morning, and the party was nearing the border between Hume and Elvenna by midday. Finnian marched in formation with the rest of his battalion, and boredom was starting to get the better of him. Being selected for the royal guard was an enormous honor, and he had been ecstatic when hearing the news.

However, his excitement turned to chagrin over time as he eventually learned that service as a royal guard was actually quite dull. Out of all the positions a soldier could be placed, the royal guards were among the least likely to ever see combat. Finnian had been a royal guard for nearly a year now, and he had never even seen an Orc during this time. He wanted nothing more than to meet these wretched brutes in battle and start making these savages pay for all the pain their people have caused.

Finnian continued marching and admired the towering green trees of the surrounding forest. The trees were getting larger in size, so he knew the Hume-Elvenna border must be getting close. He had seen these Elven trees several times in his life, but they never failed to amaze him. Their trunks were large enough for five full-grown men to stand arm to arm together and still not able to wrap their arms around it. Their limbs produced broad green leaves nearly five feet in diameter, and they emitted a sweet, fruity smell that almost filled you with a sense of euphoria as you passed by.

Finnian was drawing in a deep breath to savor the smell of the trees when he suddenly heard the startling *clank* of heavy arrows slamming into the plates of armor worn by his fellow guards.

Orcs have immense physical strength, nearly twice that of an average Human. Aside from their strength, they are also a full six to eight inches taller, and they know how to use their size and strength to their advantage. Their natural strength makes the Orcovan archer absolutely devastating. The draw weight of their bows surpasses anything a Human can pull; therefore the speed and weight of their arrows give them the ability to often penetrate the armor worn by the Humans. The Humans did design heavier plate armor capable of withstanding Orcovan bows, but the extra weight significantly affected the soldiers' mobility and the prototype was abandoned. Human soldiers' only main defense against Orc archers were their shields.

The startling sound made Finnian instinctively ready his shield and kneel low to the ground. Though he was fortunate enough to not have been hit by the first volley, at least forty other guards sank to the ground and never got back up. Another heavy volley of arrows followed shortly after, and ten to fifteen more dropped. Arrows continued to rain down upon them, and a group of roughly fifty Orcs emerged from the surrounding forest and poured onto the travelers.

Orcs often patrolled their own borders with companies of this size, and they never passed up an opportunity to attack their enemies, even when they were outnumbered. Orcs were aggressive and confident, and not without reason.

Finnian heard several officers begin to shout orders to form the line and protect the carriage, though the orders were altogether unnecessary. Royal guards were highly trained and knew exactly what they needed to do without having been told. Their reaction was essentially muscle memory for them.

The royal guards on foot surrounded the carriage, while the guards on horseback charged the oncoming attackers. The foot soldiers linked their shields side by side to create a protective wall, and they thrust their spears at the oncoming attackers as they approached.

The steel in Orcovan armor was, as one would imagine, quite heavy and not penetrable by the spear thrust of a man, but Hume trained its soldiers to exploit the weaknesses in their enemies' armor. Their first target was always to be the neck, between the Orc's helm and chest plate. There was a large enough gap here to make for the easy entrance of a spear when in the hands of an experienced soldier.

Orcs' preferred melee weapon was a poleaxe, for it provided them with a lot of leverage to take full advantage of their superior strength. Their fighting style was extremely aggressive, and they simply relied on their heavy armor for protection.

The bulk of the Orcovan archers aimed for the royal carriage. After only a few short moments, the vehicle resembled a pincushion, but it was lined with steel plating for this very reason. The royal family was well-protected. The Orcovan archers eventually halted their firing and began to join their comrades in the assault on the royal carriage.

The Orcs' poleaxes crashed down on the guards' shields, but they managed to hold the line. Human archers had started firing at the Orcovan raiders, though their arrows were less effective than the Orcs'.

Finnian tightened his grip on his shield as he prepared for a heavy downward blow from a poleaxe. The impact felt like an entire tree had landed on his shield, and he barely had the strength to keep his hold on the grip. He quickly recovered from the blow, and he realized the Orc's poleaxe was stuck in his shield. Finnian immediately sprang into action when he realized his advantage. Before the Orc could pry the axe loose, Finnian jolted forward and thrust his spear toward the opening in the Orc's armor at the neck. He slightly missed his target and hit the top of the Orc's chest plate instead, but the spear glanced upward and sank deep into the Orc's flesh. The Orc let out a muffled cry of pain and folded onto the ground, grasping at his neck. Finnian quickly withdrew his spear, pried the axe from his shield, and braced himself for the next attacker.

Finnian could feel the surge of adrenaline as he struggled to hold the line with his fellow guards. He had timed his spear thrusts well and had killed two more Orcs and wounded at least another two or three. Finnian later recalled the adrenaline rush of combat feeling like a drug. What started as fear gave way to intense thrill and excitement. He had waited so long and had been bottling up his hatred for the Orcs for too long now.

He saw an Orc charging in his direction with his axe raised and ready to strike. He braced himself for the impact, but it never came. The swing which he thought was aimed at him came crashing down on the helmet of the soldier immediately to his left, splitting open his skull. The man buckled to the ground instantly without making so much as a sound.

Finnian yelled, "Break in the wall! Break in the wall!" and soldiers from the rear tried to push forward, but it was too late. The Orcs pushed their way through the opening and everything was immediate chaos. Finnian threw his spear at the oncoming attackers and quickly drew his hand-and-a-half sword.

He charged the nearest Orc and slammed him with his shield, but Finnian would have guessed that he had instead just charged into a stone wall. *Wow, these guys are strong!* he thought. However, his hasty tactic had been effective. The Orc hadn't been paying attention to Finnian, and the shield bash took him off guard, causing him to stumble. It only took a moment for Finnian to realize this, and he immediately took advantage of it. He thrust his sword directly into the opening in the armpit of his enemy's armor. Almost half of the sword's blade sank into the chest cavity, and the Orc collapsed on the ground.

Finnian felt another surge of adrenaline, pulled his sword out of the body of his fallen enemy, and continued fighting.

The sounds of screaming and clashing of steel were almost deafening. Finnian wasn't sure what to expect, but he had never expected combat to be this chaotic.

Both the Humans and the Orcovans were taking heavy losses. Finnian just barely dodged a vertical swing of a poleaxe, and the blade sliced straight down the face of his helmet, lacerating his left eyebrow. He felt no pain, but he knew he was injured because he could see nothing but blood in his left eye. He tried to ignore his injury, but the steel of his helmet had been folded inward from the blow and it was repeatedly poking his laceration. He had no choice; he threw off his helmet and continued fighting.

As the battle progressed, the Orcovan numbers were dwindling. More than three-quarters of them had fallen. One Orc managed to push through the guards and reached the royal carriage. The carriage was completely enclosed with two doors that bolted from the inside, but these bolts were no match for the strength of an Orc.

He jumped onto the carriage and began heaving against the bolted door. Finnian saw this and sprinted toward the vehicle. By the time he reached it, the Orcovan had just broken the latch on the door and he swung it open. Queen Evelyn let out a terrified scream, and the Orcovan began to step into the carriage, drawing his secondary weapon, a longsword. King Aidan started to rise from his seat as he drew a dagger to lunge at the intruder in a desperate attempt to protect his family.

Just as Aidan rose to his feet and the Orc's sword was pulled clear of its scabbard, a blade burst through the front of the Orc's neck and bright red blood spilled onto the floor of the carriage. The sword in his neck withdrew as suddenly as it had appeared, and he started grasping futilely at his profusely bleeding neck as his knees began to buckle. A man's hand reached around the Orc's helmet and pulled him backward, out of the threshold of the carriage. The Orc landed on the ground with a heavy *thud* as the royal family stared in shock at a young man, face covered in blood from a laceration on his eyebrow, standing before them trying to catch his breath.

He surveyed the family, and once he was satisfied that nobody inside was injured, he slammed the broken door shut and continued fighting, being sure he was never further two or three paces from the carriage.

The fighting continued to rage until there was a loud blast from a horn. The few remaining Orcovans quickly withdrew and retreated into the forest. Finnian stood outside the carriage, panting in exhaustion. He stuck the blade of his sword into the ground and used it for support as he watched the Orcs withdraw. He was impressed with the speed and efficiency with which they responded to the order.

He had a newfound respect for these enemies. Their tactics, their organization, their discipline—it all rivaled the best soldiers Hume had to offer. They were obviously very disciplined and well-trained, something he never expected of the "dumb, brutish Orcs."

The reality is that the Orcovans have a comparable level of intelligence to Humans, despite their rugged behemoth exterior. This is quickly apparent to anyone who meets an Orc on the battlefield, for they are disciplined, calculating, and their tactics would impress even the finest officers of Hume.

The people of Orcova generally have a darker complexion when compared to the other Andruvian races, with their skin tone ranging from gray to a darker brown. Their faces have a distinct swine-like appearance, with their noses and mouths extend outward from the face by two to three inches, and their noses are upturned, exposing their vertical slit nostrils. Both their top and bottom canines extend roughly one inch beyond the rest of their teeth, forming four small fangs that protrude slightly when their mouths are closed. It is customary in their culture for every male to shave his head when he reaches military age, which occurs at the age of seventeen years. The women, however, will grow their thick black hair out to at least shoulder length and keep it in an ornamental braid. Besides their facial features, complexion, and size, there are no other differences in anatomy when compared to Humans.

In fact, many have proposed that Orcs, Humans, Elves, and Dwarves may all share a common ancestry, though there are just as many others who reject this theory. Unfortunately, no one knows for sure, and it is a topic of debate among historians.

Finnian stood near the carriage, panting heavily as he watched the last of the Orcs disappear into the forest. He looked around him, seeing numerous bodies piled on top of one another, with various screams and moans from the injured. His heart sank in his stomach when he realized how few of the royal guards were left. His battalion had almost four hundred men when they left Enlanor, Hume's capital city, and less than seventy-five remained.

Finnian was speechless. *I thought the royal guards were some of the best soldiers in the Human army! How could this happen!* he thought. He began to feel foolish for his naivete. Never again would he be so cavalier in his attitude toward the Orcs.

Among the wounded were both Humans and Orcs, although none of the wounded Orcs survived long enough to be taken captive. Mercy for a wounded enemy was unheard of among Orcs, and the Humans thought they'd return the favor. They loaded the wounded Humans onto what remained of the horses for the trip back to Enlanor.

A group of guards opened the carriage doors to check on the royal family, and thankfully none of them were injured. The carriage was still roadworthy, and it was swiftly turned around and started back toward Enlanor. The trip had proved to be too dangerous, and the remaining guards wanted nothing more than to get the royal family back to the safety of the city walls.

The return trip home was uneventful, and the remaining guards concluded that the group of Orcs must have stumbled upon them by happenstance. Every one of the guards breathed a sigh of relief as they traveled over the crest of a hill and the city came into view. They didn't have the energy or the numbers for another fight. As soon as the royal carriage arrived at Enlanor, King Aidan jumped out and began searching through the crowd of the guards. He was searching for the "boy with the cut on his face." He made his way through the group and finally came face-to-face with Finnian, recognizing him instantly.

"You! You're the one who saved me and my family from that Orc!" exclaimed Aidan. He threw his arms around Finnian and said, "Thank you, my boy! Well done!"

Finnian was frozen. He had no idea what he was supposed to do. The king of Hume hugging one of the royal guards was highly irregular. He also felt a little self-conscious, for he was covered in sweat and blood, and he reasoned that he must have smelled awful. This was not the way he would have liked to officially meet the king of Hume. Despite all this, Finnian was put at ease by Aidan's demeanor.

Aidan had a friendly yet confident charm about him, and he had a way with people. He was very gifted at making others feel at ease, and this was one of the reasons he was so well-liked and respected by those closest to him. He was a handsome, rugged man of forty-seven, with short graying hair and kind brown eyes. His face was clean-shaven and had a strong jawline. If anyone ever had a regal, kingly look to them, it was Aidan. His poise and overall appearance were almost cliché for a king.

Aidan had served in the Human army until the death of his father, Nolan, at which time he became Hume's current king. Aidan was a gifted soldier, and although he now had the greater responsibility of leading his province, he was still a soldier at heart and longed for the battlefield. In fact, his family had to convince him not to step out of the carriage and join the action with the guards. Since becoming king of Hume, Aidan always insisted that he be on the battlefield with his troops. How could anyone expect to lead an army and ask them to risk their lives for their king if he refused to be out there with them?

Aidan pulled back, keeping his hands on Finnian's shoulders, and said, What is your name, son?"

Finnian tried to speak, but only a crackling whisper came out. He was parched and could feel his tongue sticking to the roof of his mouth. He cleared his throat and tried again.

"My name is Finnian, my king," he said, and he gave a slight bow.

"Well, Finnian, I am forever in your debt. Thank you!" Aidan motioned with his head. "Come! Meet my family!"

Finnian was still somewhat in shock as they walked over to the carriage. After arriving, Aidan motioned to the queen and said, "Finnian, this is my wife, Evelyn."

Finnian bowed and said, "It's an honor, my queen."

Evelyn approached him, took his hands in hers, and said, "No, the honor is mine. You saved our lives! I don't know how we could ever thank you!"

Evelyn was a very beautiful soft-spoken woman of the same age as Aidan. She had long auburn hair and soft green eyes. Her stature was shorter than average for women in Hume, and like her husband, she too had the ability to make one feel at ease when speaking to her. She didn't carry herself like one would expect a queen to carry herself, and this is mainly due to the fact that she was not raised as a noble. She identified more with the common man because that is exactly the environment she was raised in.

Aidan motioned to the boy standing next to Evelyn. "And this is our son, Owen."

Finnian bowed again.

Owen was a quiet thirteen-year-old boy with brown hair and eyes. He only volunteered a quiet "Thank you" to Finnian.

Owen's thanks were genuine, but he wasn't yet comfortable speaking in public. Plus, he was still slightly shaken up from the events of the battle. The image of the sword slicing through the Orc's neck in the carriage had been replaying through his mind the entire ride back to Enlanor, and the fact that his shoes were covered in the Orc's blood didn't help the matter.

"And lastly, this is our daughter, Reagan," said Aidan.

Finnian again bowed and said, "It's a pleasure, my lady." Reagan said nothing, but she gave a very bright smile to Finnian.

Reagan was twenty years old and resembled a younger version of her mother, though she was taller than Evelyn. She took more after Aidan in that regard. She had vibrant auburn hair and green eyes, and Finnian noticed some slight freckling on the bridge of her nose and on her cheeks. He was quite taken aback by how beautiful this girl was, and he became embarrassed and flustered when he realized he was staring. Aidan had noticed it as well . . .

Hume had done away with laws that prohibit the royal family from only marrying other members of a royal family during the reign of King Nolan, Aidan's father. Nolan had instilled the same philosophy about marriage in Aidan, which is why he married Evelyn, the daughter of a humble stonemason. As Reagan's father, he still had the right to arrange a husband for her; however, he doubted he would ever be able to bring himself to do it. He married the one he loved, and he and Evelyn always intended for their children to do the same.

Aidan considered the prospect of this young man taking a liking to his daughter and concluded he wanted to get to know the boy better. He finally said, "Finnian, get that wound cleaned, bathe, and rest. Tonight, you will join me and my family for dinner!"

Finnian's heart began to beat almost as heavily as it did during the battle. The thought of eating dinner with the royal family filled him with anxiety. He was a soldier, albeit a quite inexperienced one, but what did he know about proper palace etiquette? He wanted to decline the offer, but it occurred to him that it wasn't exactly an offer. Aidan had said it so matter-of-factly that it felt more like an order from his king. Several of the other royal guards standing nearby exchanged surprised looks. Aidan's generosity was well-known, but inviting a royal guard to dine with his family was unprecedented.

Finnian stammered, "Uh . . . Erm . . . Yes, my king. I would be honored to."

"Excellent! Go get your rest. I will send for you later this evening," concluded Aidan.

Finnian bowed once more, and Aidan and his family went into the palace.

The guards all crowded around Finnian and started laughing and congratulating him. One of the guards said, "Not bad for a rookie!" and ruffled Finnian's hair with his hand, accidentally splitting apart the dried blood over his left eyebrow.

Fresh blood began running down his face. Finnian winced while gingerly touching his laceration and said, "I think I better go get this wound cleaned and dressed." His sergeant dismissed him, and he left for the infirmary in his barracks.

~

Finnian let out a quiet laugh. He was just a boy then. Of course, that was only four years ago, but to Finnian, it felt as though four decades had passed since then.

Through discipline and excessive training, he had grown to be a very skilled warrior. In fact, he was one of the finest swordsmen in Hume. He had become very close to the royal family, and he had more than his battlefield accomplishments to thank for that.

Aidan grew very fond of Finnian, and the two had spent much time together over the past four years. Spending as much time at the palace as Finnian did, he and Reagan took an interest in one another as well. At times, Finnian almost felt pushed to spend more time with Regan by both of her parents, but especially Aidan. In truth, Aidan had long thought that Finnian would make a great son-in-law, and he was just the type of man he would want to marry his daughter, for Finnian was much like Aidan himself.

With as much time as the two had spent together, Finnian was still reluctant to ask for Reagan's hand in marriage due to his vocation. He felt he would never have been the accomplished soldier he was if his attention were divided. He also had to admit he was a bit frightened at the idea of becoming a prince. First and foremost, Finnian was a soldier, and a very fine one at that. He loved Reagan, of that there was no doubt, but he still longed for the thrill of combat. He had a gift for it, and he felt it almost irresponsible to waste that gift. Finnian had long felt the Orcs deserved to pay for the deaths of his parents, along with the countless other atrocities they had committed, and who better to demand that payment than him? Becoming a husband and a prince would certainly limit his ability to serve Hume with the battle prowess which he had in excess.

Finnian was promoted after the battle with the Orcovan raiding party four years ago, and he continued to climb in rank over the next couple of years. He eventually became a captain in the royal guard battalion, but he requested to be transferred shortly thereafter. Since combat is not something a royal guard sees much of, he asked to be reassigned as a patrol officer, and because of his skills in battle, there was little objection to his transfer request.

The patrol branch of the Human army is tasked with continuous monitoring of the roads in Hume for any sign of threats, and they see the most enemy encounters of any branch of the Human army, which is precisely what Finnian desired. Platoons are on weekly rotations: one week at the outpost, patrolling the roads, then one week in Enlanor. There were a total of four outposts in Hume: north, south, east, and west. Finnian was assigned to the northern patrol. Because the northeast border is shared with Orcova, the likelihood of encountering the enemy is greater there than in any other location.

The week spent at the capital did include some light patrolling around the city, but it was primarily a week of recuperation. Weeks at the outpost were spent patrolling approximately thirty-mile routes every day, which could be quite grueling. There were always at least three platoons at each outpost that would patrol the roads in their perspective regions.

Over the past year, Orcovan encounters were getting too common for comfort. They had grown increasingly aggressive toward Human patrols, and their presence in the country was growing more and more frequent.

Patrol captains would not typically be out with the platoon on a routine patrol, but Finnian never passed up the chance to be out in the field. An entire platoon being used for a standard patrol was usually not necessary, but three ten-man patrols had gone missing within the past month. As a result, the decision was made to start sending fifty-man platoons on patrol across Hume.

Today had been quiet, with no signs of Orcs. Galen, Finnian's closest friend and most trusted lieutenant, rode up alongside him.

"Can you believe this heat?" asked Finnian.

Galen answered, "It's pretty brutal. This armor is so hot, I feel like I'm being cooked in an oven. I'd say I'm about cooked all the way through by now."

Finnian laughed. "Yes? I *am* getting pretty hungry, but lucky for you we need to keep moving. Our rotation is up and there's a council meeting tonight. I want to get the platoon back to Enlanor as quickly as we can in case there's an incident."

"This close to the city?" replied Galen. "The Orcs have never come that far into the country before."

Finnian shrugged. "Maybe not, but having all the rulers of the Union together in one place would be the best time for them to try it."

Galen nodded and said, "Most likely, but we have so many soldiers patrolling Northern Hume that there is no way they'd get to Enlanor without us knowing about it."

Finnian looked at Galen and replied, "Are you willing to take that chance?"

Galen laughed. "Yes, but you know me, Finnian! Like I've told you, this is my last year in active duty. I'm going to retire, find a nice girl, and settle down. If you ask me, that's taking a bigger chance than staying with what's familiar!"

Finnian jokingly scoffed and said, "Don't remind me. It's bad enough that Hume will be losing a gifted soldier, but I also have to find someone new to push around!"

Galen gestured to the soldiers riding behind them and said, "Well, take your pick!"

Both men laughed and brought their horses back into a slow gallop and the rest of the platoon followed down the road toward Enlanor.

2

T HE YEAR WAS 1127 of the Fourth Age. The continent of Andruvia is one with a long, bloody history, and it has been at war almost constantly since its beginning. War is simply a part of life for its inhabitants. In fact, there have been very few generations throughout history that had ever seen peace.

The continent came to be known as "Andruvia" long before the boundary lines of its provinces were drawn, though the exact origin of this name is unknown. Folklore tells of an advanced, prosperous mother race called "Andruvians," whose descendants eventually segregated and formed most of the modern-day races. However, the recording of history was not common practice until the start of the First Age, and much of the events prior to the First Age have been lost to history.

Some documents predating the First Age do exist, though their authenticity and accuracy are still debated. The debating is largely due to the undeniable discontinuity between documents. Furthermore, there are others that contain stories that are almost certainly fictional and were only told for entertainment. Thus, no one can be sure which documents are reliable, and the inclusion of them in scholarly discussion is unheard of.

There are six known provinces in Andruvia, and the current borders of each province are determined by the major rivers of the continent. In the center of the continent is the plains and lakes region of Hume, home of the Humans. Hume is a land with fertile soil that provides more than half of Andruvia's crop supply. Its many freshwater lakes also make it the primary supplier of fish. The value of Hume due to its food supply alone makes it perhaps the most valuable piece of land in all of Andruvia.

To the northeast lies the mountainous province of Orcova, home of the "Orcs," as the Humans would say, though its inhabitants view that name as derogatory and prefer to be called Orcovans. They are one of the most belligerent races in Andruvia, and their hostility toward other races has always centered around greed. They want more land. They want the fertile soil of Hume, the rich mineral and ore deposits of Dwarvonia, and the plentiful hardwood supply of the Elvenna forests. The climate and conditions of Orcova are such that it can barely support their population, and expanding their regime will take more resources than their homeland can offer. They are an ambitious people who refuse to be stifled by the other races, and they have stubbornly stuck to their manifesto of expansion for the last one thousand years.

To the northwest lies the lush, forested province of Elvenna, home of the Elves. Elves are roughly the same height as humans, but they are leaner and have less muscle mass. As a result, they are physically weaker, but they are also among the fastest and most agile of the Andruvian races, making them very dangerous swordsmen. Elves also have very keen eyesight, enabling them to see small details at farther distances and also see better in darker environments. They have a lighter complexion than the average Human, slightly larger and pointed ears, and have vertically slit pupils similar to that of a cat. Their hair colors range as widely as that of Humans, but their hair is very fine and always grows straight. It is very rare for an Elf to have the ability to grow any kind of facial hair. Those that can are often accused of being "mixed-blooded," meaning they have some Human ancestry, though this has never been proven. Otherwise, their physical appearance is similar to that of Humans.

During the Second Age, a boundary dispute between Hume and Elvenna escalated into a small-scale war. The Humans didn't want to give up a portion of the Elvennan forest because of their need for hardwood, but the Elves see the entire forest as their home and felt that the Humans had no right to it. Several battles were fought along the border, but neither country desired a full-scale war over the matter. The kings of each province met in a council to discuss the disputed boundary, and the decision was eventually made to draw the border along the Siria River. Both agreed that each province had valuable resources to offer the other, so Hume would surrender their claim to the Elven forest in exchange for trading their crops and fish for hardwood. This treaty between the Humans and the Elves was called the "Andruvian Union," and as time went on, each race began to consider the other as basically their own countrymen.

To the southwest lies the marshlands of Aquaria, which is inhabited by the elusive Aquarians. Over the generations, Aquarians adapted to life in a marsh. They developed the ability to hold their breath for at least one hour and are very proficient swimmers. Their hands and feet are broad and strong, giving them excellent propulsion in the water. Their complexion is unique; almost light blue in color. Otherwise, Aquarians are overall are very similar to Humans in appearance, and a common ancestry between the two races is generally accepted.

The Aquarians were once a more prominent race in Andruvia, but they have lived in seclusion and obscurity ever since they were defeated in the war with the Humans during the late First Age. Aquaria was once included as a territory of Hume, but the Aquarians always felt as though they were considered to be second-class citizens, and Cormac, the Human king, never led with their best interest in mind. Beyond that, the Aquarians also coveted the fertile farmland and abundant freshwater lakes of Hume.

The growing tensions eventually resulted in a civil war, which lasted several years, and though the Aquarians surprised the Humans with their zeal and determination, the tide of the war eventually began to favor the Humans. Despite their inevitable loss of the war, the Aquarians refused to surrender.

Not wanting to decimate the entire population of Aquaria, Cormac eventually decided to grant their secession from Hume on two conditions: There would be peace between the two provinces thereafter, and Aquaria had to pay an annual tax to Hume. In truth, Aquaria contributed little to the Human economy, but continuing the conflict promised little reward for Hume. The decision was criticized by many, but Cormac maintained that there was little to gain from decimating the Aquarian population, and they would still receive at least *some* benefit from Aquaria's tributes.

The Aquarians accepted, and though they finally had the independence they wanted, they struggled to build the empire they saw themselves being. The two countries have remained at peace since then, but their relations have always been sour. They were usually faithful in their tax contribution to Hume, but more recently their contributions have been getting increasingly lower and typically past the deadline. As a result, the relationship between the two provinces is nearing a breaking point once again.

Directly to the south lies the desert province of Serpenta, a region few ever venture into. The scorching heat and having little water present a deadly challenge for any traveler, but the environment is the least of a traveler's worries. The greater danger of Serpenta is its mysterious inhabitants, the snakelike Serpens. Serpens have the lower body of a snake with a manlike upper body. They have two arms that are anatomically similar to Humans, with four-fingered hands. Their heads also resemble that of a snake and have pale yellow eyes with slit pupils. The length of a full-grown adult is approximately thirty feet, and they are able to move very, very quickly. Encounters with these people are always hostile, with the victor usually being the Serpen. They will defend their borders with unrivaled ferocity, but not once has a Serpen ever been spotted outside of their own country. Not much is known about these people or their culture. Most attempts to contact them would typically end up with one being impaled by their spears or crushed by their constricting bodies. Perhaps the most famous attempt to contact these people occurred in the early Fourth Age when a brave Human ambassador rode into the Serpentan Desert flying a white flag and carrying no weapons of any kind. As the sun rose the following morning, the Human border patrol found the ambassador's flag dyed completely red with blood, planted in the sand at the edge of the border. The ambassador was nowhere to be found, and his body has never been recovered to this day. The message was clear: There is no white flag with Serpens. Do not enter Serpenta under any circumstances.

What lies south of Serpenta is a mystery known only to the Serpens themselves. There are three known documents predating the First Age that speak of a lush jungle south of the desert inhabited by a birdlike race of people. These tales have fascinated Andruvians for generations; however, there is one document from the early First Age that tells of a party of Elves that traveled to the southernmost point of the Serpentan Desert and found only ocean. Most scholars consider the latter story to be the truth, but the matter is still debated to this day. Unfortunately, the Serpens have not allowed anyone to venture into the desert to confirm the stories.

The rocky terrain of Dwarvonia that lies to the east is home to the rugged Dwarves. Dwarves are short, roughly two-thirds the height of humans, but they have slightly greater physical strength. They have thick, muscular arms and legs and a broad chest. Their robust physical makeup is almost comical when paired with their short stature. Their complexion and hair color are comparable to Humans, although their hair tends to be thick and bristly. Regardless of gender, it is rare to ever see a Dwarf with head or facial hair due to the difficulty of maintaining it. Most Dwarves begin shaving their children's heads after birth, and the practice continues throughout their entire lives. Besides the difference in height and muscle mass, there are no other physical features that distinguish them from Humans.

They are a stern and assertive people, but they are loyal and dependable to their very core. There is an old proverb in Hume that reads, "The road to a Dwarven friendship is riddled with many sharp stones, but the destination is one that shall be written in stone."

During the Third Age, Dwarvonia declared war with the Andruvian Union over a trade dispute. The Dwarven culture centered heavily around mining, and their homeland was a rich supplier of a variety of ores and minerals. Dwarvonia provided the union with their mined ore and minerals in exchange for hardwood and crops, but the Dwarves felt the deal heavily favored the union, and the negotiations eventually became hostile. The war lasted almost seven years and was one of the costliest wars Andruvia has seen to date. Even against the combined strength of Elvenna and Hume, the Dwarves proved they were not to be trifled with.

As the war was nearing its end, the Dwarves were running low on resources, especially food. Rather than let his people starve, the

Dwarven king requested an audience with the union's leaders to negotiate the terms of a peace treaty. The union eventually agreed to give Dwarvonia a fairer compensation for their ore and minerals, and Dwarvonia became a member of the Andruvian Union. Their entrance into the union marked the beginning of the Fourth Age.

The relationships between the races in the Andruvian Union has since blossomed into one of mutual respect and admiration. Trade disputes are now uncommon, and any disputes that do occur are settled quickly and professionally. More importantly, the provinces in the union enjoy the benefit of having allies in a continent as war-torn as Andruvia, which proved to be especially crucial when the war with the brutal Orcovans erupted during the Fourth Age.

~

All members of the Andruvian Union Council were present, and the session was about to begin. Council meetings would be held twice per year, and the three participating provinces would rotate hosting the session. This current session was being hosted by Hume. Each province had two members on the council: The king of the province and the commander, who was the highest-ranking official in the province's army.

The meetings would typically begin with discussions of the allocation of each province's resources. Majority of the discussion revolved around the distribution of horses from Hume. Due to its terrain, abundant food sources, and flat plains, Hume is where most of the horses in Andruvia are bred, raised, and trained. Without the superior cavalry of the Andruvian Union, the war with Orcova would be going very differently.

There is no denying that the Orcs have the better warriors. They are bigger, stronger, more resilient, and have superior archers. The only advantage the union has is their vastly superior cavalry. The climate and terrain of Orcova make breeding and training passable warhorses quite difficult, and as a result, the Orcovan Army lacks a proper cavalry.

This is the sole reason for Hume being Orcova's primary target since the start of the war.

After the trade discussions had ended, it was the time for military discussions. Connor, the Human commander, had been eager to start.

He began, "We have a situation in Hume. In the last month, three of our ten-man patrols have vanished without a trace. There have been no bodies, no horses . . . no clues of any kind. We have been forced to send groups as large as a company of fifty soldiers just to patrol our own roads." Connor paused. He cleared his throat, then continued, "If I may be candid, my friends, something doesn't feel right about this. Our patrols have been attacked on a fairly regular basis since the Orcs started getting bolder and are coming into our country more frequently, but they have never done anything like this before. If Orcs kill a patrol, they are more than pleased to desecrate the bodies by hanging them from the trees or dismembering them to try to frighten us. They are very proud of their kills and make every effort to show them off. But this . . . this is different. Our men simply disappeared without a trace. No bodies, no weapons, no armor . . . nothing." Connor shifted his gaze between the Elves and the Dwarves. "Have you noticed any strange occurrences in your provinces?"

The Elves and the Dwarves exchanged puzzled looks.

Oleg, the Dwarven king, finally said, "No, Connor, we've had nothing like that. There have been a few Orc raiding parties, but nothing out of the ordinary. Perhaps they are starting to change their tactics? Try their hand at stealth?"

Oleg glanced at the two Elves sitting next to him, the experts of stealth tactics.

Gildir, the Elven commander, responded, "It's of course possible, but very idiosyncratic for them. They've used the same tactics since the very start of this war, and it's been effective. Even with all three of our provinces fighting, we still struggle to win every single fight. Why would they change their tactics when it isn't necessary?"

Gildir shifted his gaze to Connor. "I'm sorry, Connor, but we haven't experienced anything like this in Elvenna, either. But I think you're making the correct choice by increasing the size of your patrols.

Are there any other abnormalities besides the patrols that have gone missing?"

Connor shook his head. "No, nothing else out of the ordinary. Our patrols encounter the usual small parties using guerrilla tactics, but we've been quite successful at repelling them lately. They aren't pushing too hard. It would seem they're testing our defenses. All of our patrols have been warned to expect the worst."

Everyone in the room nodded in agreement. Everyone was thinking the same thing, but no one dared to say it aloud. The Orcovans are just prodding the Human defenses to test for weaknesses. The Hume-Orcova border is too large to station enough troops along its entirety, and eventually the Orcs will find the weakest spot in Hume's defenses. An invasion is likely on the horizon.

3

FINNIAN WAS A bit too optimistic about the travel time back
to Enlanor. By the time he and the platoon had arrived, the
meeting had almost concluded.

As the platoon was entering the city gates, Galen turned to Finnian
and jokingly said, "It's a good thing we rushed here. The council would
have been doomed if we hadn't!"

Finnian laughed and replied, "With your swordsman skills, they
would have been doomed either way!"

Galen made a snort of derision. "Just name the time and the place
and I'll teach you a thing or two about using a sword!"

Both of the men laughed. Galen was quite comfortable with a
sword, but there was no denying that Finnian was the finer swordsman.
In fact, Galen had never beaten Finnian in the years they had sparred
together.

Finnian dismounted his house and reported to Major Brady's office.
Major Brady was a fifty-two-year-old seasoned combat veteran. The
man was tall, brawny, and tougher than nails. He was a man of few
words and wasn't a fan of exchanging pleasantries. Finnian couldn't
even recall a single moment where he ever witnessed Brady smile.

He knocked on Brady's office door and heard the major's gruff
voice say, "Yes?"

Finnian stepped into the office and stood at attention before the
desk for what felt like a whole minute. The major finally looked up from
his paperwork and stared at Finnian. He said nothing, but he didn't
need to. Finnian knew it was now his time to talk.

Finnian began, "Captain Finnian reporting in. No incidents, Major.
No Orcovan signs or encounters, all my men are well and accounted
for."

Major Brady nodded and said, "Very good, Captain. You and your men are dismissed for the night." After he was finished speaking, Brady went back to his desk work.

"Thank you, Major," replied Finnian, and he left his office. Finnian dismissed his men, bathed in the barracks, and put on a fresh set of civilian clothes. For that, he was thankful. His armor was of course necessary, but nothing feels better than taking your armor off at the end of a long, hot day.

Finnian left the barracks and went directly to the palace. At that moment, there was only one person Finnian wanted to see.

He walked up to the front palace gate and gave a friendly nod to the guards as he walked through the entrance.

"Good evening, Captain," one of them responded.

Finnian had spent so much time at the palace in the last several years that the guards allowed him passage as if he were a member of the royal family. Not only that, King Aidan had also ordered all the palace guards to allow Finnian passage at any time.

Finnian walked into the foyer of the palace and almost ran into Prince Owen as he had been walking by.

"Finnian! It's good to see you!" said Owen as he leaned in to hug him. He was now a tall, very thin, seventeen-year-old. He had just begun to grow facial hair, but it was still quite thin and patchy. His sister constantly teased him for it, but Owen still wore his thin red beard with pride.

Being a member of the royal family, Owen was exempt from training at the academy, though he did still have the option. Aidan told him on his fifteenth birthday that it was completely his decision whether to enter the academy, and he would never interfere or be upset if Owen chose not to go. Historically, most princes of Hume chose not to go to the academy, but Aidan was an exception. He enlisted the very day he turned fifteen years old, and he has actively served in the army ever since.

Queen Evelyn didn't relish the idea of both her husband and her son riding off to battle, and it was for her sake that Owen had decided not to go. It was a decision that haunted him almost daily. He often tried to convince himself that Hume has plenty of good soldiers and his country needed its heir to the throne to stay safe, especially considering the fact that the king was already out on the battlefield. Even so, he was too much like his father. How could a leader ask his men to risk their lives while he was safe and sound within his palace?

"It's good to see you too," answered Finnian. Each of the men broke the hug and stepped back, facing one another. Finnian looked Owen up and down and said, "Owen, how do you expect to ever wear a crown on your head without any muscles on your body to support the extra weight?!"

Owen laughed and responded, "Oh, I can always get stronger. But you . . . you'll never get any taller. If only you *could*, you would have slain *twice* as many Orcs by now!"

"Ha!" replied Finnian. "Why don't you join me in the next battle, and we'll see who bags more Orcs!"

Owen's smiled faded. He had confided in Finnian in the past about his struggle with staying out of the army, and Finnian realized that he had just inadvertently struck a nerve.

He was about to apologize when Queen Evelyn walked into the foyer.

"Finnian! I didn't expect to see you tonight! Didn't you just return from your rotation today?"

"I did, and even though I'm fond of the men I fight with, I decided I had seen enough of their faces over the past week and need a change of scenery!"

Evelyn laughed and said, "Right . . . and I'm sure the change of scenery you have in mind can be found in the library. She isn't expecting you, so it will be a nice surprise."

Finnian tried to act surprised and said, "What! Reagan isn't the *only* reason I come to the palace!"

Owen jokingly scoffed. "Well, she's the *main* reason, anyway!"

Finnian was trying to think of a witty comeback when Evelyn laughed again and nudged Finnian in the direction of the library.

Finnian began walking down the hall toward the library, and as he walked, a memory from two years ago came to his mind . . .

The night Aidan invited Finnian to dinner with his family after the Orcovan ambush four years ago had been one of the most terrifying experiences of Finnian's life, which is saying a lot for a soldier. He was raised in a humble home, and he moved directly from there to the academy. He hadn't the slightest idea of what proper dinner etiquette was when dining with royalty.

Fortunately for him, Aidan and his family are very gracious and charitable toward their guests. Overall, Aidan's family was more in touch with the struggles of life that most Humans faced. Aidan's father, Nolan, made it a priority to instill into him the idea that a king can't effectively govern and care for his people if he is out of touch with the struggles that his people face. Evelyn, on the other hand, needed no lessons on the life of the people because she was raised in that environment.

Aidan did most of the talking during dinner, and as much as Finnian tried to concentrate on the conversation, he couldn't help but be distracted by the beautiful auburn-haired princess sitting across the dining table from him.

Aidan saw a lot of himself in Finnian, and he liked him immediately. From then on, the two spent a lot of time together, and dinner invitations with the royal family became a regular occurrence. The two would sharpen each other's swordsman skills as they sparred together, Aidan often invited Finnian to accompany him as a "bodyguard" when attending to his kingly duties across the province, they compared their experiences in the academy, they talked about their parents, they discussed their childhoods . . . basically everything.

Aidan and Evelyn grew to love Finnian like a son. In learning about what happened to his parents, Aidan's heart broke for Finnian. So many families across Hume have a similar story, and Aidan thought that Finnian needed guidance from a father figure now more than ever. A path of vengeance is a path of pain and misery, and that is the last thing he wanted for Finnian.

Finnian's relationship with the entire royal family grew over the years, especially with Reagan. Any time Finnian had free time, if he wasn't spending it with Aidan, he was with Reagan. Though he had a strong conviction about his duty to Hume as a soldier, Finnian couldn't deny that his heart was now being pulled in two different directions. He eventually concluded that his liking for Reagan was inconsequential, for she is a princess, after all. The king couldn't possibly want his daughter marrying someone like him.

The irony of it all is that Finnian is precisely the kind of man Aidan would want to marry his daughter. Their budding romance was painfully obvious to anyone who ever saw them together. Evelyn frequently wanted to play the matchmaker between them, but she was always stopped by Aidan. "Let their relationship develop in its own timing," he would tell her. He knew that Finnian still struggled with the pain from his past and didn't want to force anything upon him, but after two years, he figured that perhaps a little nudge wouldn't hurt . . .

One evening, roughly two years after first meeting Finnian, Aidan requested his presence in the palace after he had been dismissed from his duties for the day. Finnian was led to the library by one of the palace servants, and he found Aidan reading and smoking his pipe.

As soon as Finnian entered the room, Aidan looked up and said, "Finnian! Come, sit." He put down his pipe and book and turned toward Finnian.

The smell of pipe tobacco filled Finnian's nostrils as he sat at the table, and he winced. His father smoked a pipe, and Finnian couldn't stand the smell of pipe tobacco ever since his father's death. He never had the heart to tell Aidan, for he knew how much Aidan enjoyed smoking.

Aidan continued, "I want to be candid with you, Finnian. You're turning into a fine young man and a very gifted soldier. Any father would be proud to have you as a son-in-law."

Finnian's heart began pounding in his chest as he thought, *What did he just say?*

"Are you interested in my daughter?" asked Aidan. Of course, Aidan already knew the answer, but he finally wanted to discuss the matter with Finnian.

There was a long pause. Finnian had no idea what to say. He finally spoke up. "Any man to have her would be the most fortunate man in all of Andruvia."

Aidan laughed. "Ha! I am inclined to agree with you, my boy!" Aidan leaned in close. "Listen, Finnian, I know that soldiers aren't inclined to get married . . . at least not the ones your age. Never will I pressure you to neglect your duties as the very fine soldier you are, but if there is ever a time you want to ask for Reagan's hand in marriage, you have my blessing."

Finnian was at a loss for words. He glanced downward toward his boots for a moment, then looked back up at Aidan with a slight smile. "Thank you," he said.

Aidan returned the smile and gave a single nod. He then leaned back into his chair and grabbed his pipe from its stand. He drew in a couple of puffs and said, "So, how was the day?" Finnian was relieved about the subject change.

~

As he was just finishing recalling those events, Finnian walked into the library and saw Reagan sitting in the same seat Aidan had been sitting in two years prior. She was an avid reader and could often be found in the palace library, making her way through its massive literary collection. The orange rays of the sunset beamed through the library windows, directly onto Reagan, making her auburn hair glow as if it were made of gold. She had never looked so beautiful.

Reagan noticed someone had walked into the library and looked up from her book. "Finnian!" She dropped her book on the table and ran over to him and gave him a hug. "I didn't think I'd see you until tomorrow!"

"I didn't want to wait to see you," he replied.

"I trust your rotation went well?" asked Reagan.

"Very well. The heat was brutal, but there were no signs of Orcs the entire week." Reagan gave Finnian another hug.

They spent the next hour in the library discussing events from their past week and made plans for the coming week. His conversation with her father two years ago kept replaying in Finnian's mind: *If there is ever a time you want to ask for Reagan's hand in marriage, you have my blessing.*

Finnian's mind on the matter hadn't changed. The timing simply wasn't right. Finnian was a soldier at heart, and he was one of the finest in the province. His homeland needed him. He owed it to his country and to his parents to keep fighting the Orcs. Love could wait.

Throughout their conversation, Reagan noticed that Finnian seemed distracted. She paused and asked, "Is everything all right? You seem troubled by something."

Finnian quickly snapped out of his pondering and looked at Reagan. "Oh . . . sorry. I just have a lot on my mind with the issues the patrols are facing."

Reagan knew that wasn't true. She had come to know Finnian very well. In fact, she knew she loved him. It wasn't easy, but she had resolved to remain patient and wait for the day he would ask for her hand in marriage. She wasn't going to press the issue. If Finnian hasn't proposed marriage yet, she knew he must have his reasons. She had no doubt that they would be married someday, and she had decided long ago that he was worth the wait.

Reagan thought it best to lighten the mood and change the subject. She stood at attention, putting her hands on her hips and said, "Captain Finnian, you have the princess of Hume standing in front of you, and you're more interested in daydreaming about horseback riding with a bunch of sweaty men?"

Stifling a laugh, Finnian stood and bowed very low, saying, "I wouldn't dream of it, my lady!"

"Apparently, Captain Finnian, you *would* dream of it, because you just confessed to it!" she responded.

The two burst out in laughter. Their conversation continued for some time longer until Finnian announced he must retire to the barracks. He kissed the back of her hand and bid her a good night.

4

KIERAN LOOSELY GRIPPED the reins as his horse strode down the road with the rest of his platoon. He was a twenty-one-year-old soldier in his second year of active duty in the Human army patrol. He liked military life well enough, but he hadn't yet decided if he would choose to go into the reserves at the end of his mandatory five years or stay active. His family owned a pub called "The Yellow Oak" in his northern hometown of Cliften. They had been pressuring him to join them in the family business after serving his five years in the army, but he wasn't yet convinced. He wished he could be more decisive like Donal, his friend he met when they were each assigned to the same platoon last year. Donal had true zeal and passion for military life. Every man in his family went career, and he had known at a very young age that was his future—a career of military service. Kieran envied him. In a way, he thought it would actually be nice to not have the choice. If you never had a choice, you'd never have to obsess about making the right decision.

Kieran was assigned to the southern border patrol, which suited him just fine. He had never even seen Southern Hume. Even if he decided to go into the reserves after five years and join the family business, at least he had the opportunity to experience parts of Hume he'd likely would have never otherwise seen.

The patrol started early in the morning, and it had been quiet thus far. The platoon halted when they came to the edge of a pond alongside the road. The horses needed to rest and rehydrate from this heat wave they had been having all summer.

Kieran and Donal dismounted and walked over to the tall grass along the road. Kieran never missed the opportunity to appreciate the beauty of the country . . . rolling, wide-open plains, scattered lakes, the waving of the chest-high grass as it swayed in the wind . . . it was a beautiful sight to behold—

Wait, what was that? thought Kieran. He could have sworn he saw the grass move in a very unnatural way about fifty feet in front of him. Kieran turned his head slightly to Donal. "Donal, did you see something in the grass directly in front of us just now?"

Donal focused intently on the grass for several seconds, then answered, "No. What did you see?"

"I'm not sure. The grass moved like something is hiding in it," replied Kieran.

"It's probably just an animal hiding . . . maybe a deer?"

Kieran shrugged. "Maybe . . ." but he wasn't so sure. He had seen deer in the high grass many times before, but what he saw in the corner of his eye a moment ago didn't move like a deer. He wasn't sure why, but a slight chill was running down his spine.

"Let's go have a look," Donal replied as he drew his sword from its scabbard.

There it was, the thing that made Kieran and Donal very different—Donal was brave and confident. Kieran envied Donal at that moment. He hesitated to even *follow* Donal into the grass.

The others in the platoon began to walk over to the two young soldiers when they noticed that one of them had drawn his sword and was venturing out into the tall grass.

Donal was slowly advancing when he abruptly stopped. A dark object was rising from the grass, but he couldn't tell what it was. It was a dark brown in color, smooth, and the sunlight glistened off it.

It's a head! he thought. *It . . . almost looks reptilian . . .* At that moment, Donal realized what he was looking at. He started to yell, "*Serp—!*" but his words were abruptly cut short when a spear was thrust straight through his neck, one of the places the lightweight patrol armor did not adequately protect.

It all happened in the blink of an eye. Kieran had seen Donal suddenly stop. He began to yell something when, with the speed of newly released arrow, a large, dark figure sprung from the grass and thrust a spear through the neck of his friend.

Several voices behind him yelled, "Serpens!"

Immediately, the grass began to shift violently in seven other locations as the rest of the Serpens, slithering on their bellies, began racing toward the platoon. It only took one or two seconds for them to reach the edge of the tall grass, when the huge serpentine bodies shot out toward the dumbfounded soldiers. Each Serpen had his spear thrust forward as they emerged from the grass, and each connected with their target. Seven more men fell.

The Serpens drew themselves up off their bellies like a cobra, and they stood at a height of eight to nine feet. Each had a twelve-foot spear in one hand and a large tower shield in the other.

The Serpen battle tactics were an amazing sight to behold. They would draw their upper bodies back, then suddenly shoot out like a snake striking at its prey. Snakes can strike at a distance equal to half their total body length, and the Serpens were no exception. Being thirty feet in length, they could strike at distances up to fifteen feet from their original position. Furthermore, using a twelve-foot spear as their weapon extended that reach even further.

Kieran watched as a Serpen drew back and, in a flash, sprung toward the lieutenant standing a full twenty-five feet away and ran a spear clean through his lower abdomen. The lieutenant crumpled onto the ground, screaming in pain, but the Serpen quickly finished him by slamming his shield down onto his exposed face, for the patrol helmets did not have a face guard. Resistance was futile. They were not equipped to fight these foes, and already almost half the platoon was dead. Sergeant Colm, who was now the highest-ranking officer in what was left of the platoon, screamed for all the survivors to mount up and retreat.

Kieran didn't need to be told twice. He spun around, frantically looking for his horse. There! Only seven or eight paces away! He sprinted toward the horse and mounted as quickly as he could. He dug his spurs in and retreated up the road with the surviving members of his platoon as fast as their horses could carry them.

The survivors had been riding for five minutes straight when Sergeant Colm called for everyone to halt. Most of them were on the verge of hysteria and could barely keep their composure.

One of the soldiers spoke up. "What are they doing here! They've never crossed the border into Hume before!" Another soldier added, "Did you see how fast they move! How are we supposed to fight something that fast!"

Sergeant Colm shouted, "Of course we saw how fast they were! We were all there! Now, everyone, shut your mouths! This is what we're going to do: We're going to continue riding until we reach the southern outpost. I will report to Captain Martin and he will instruct us from there. We obviously do not have the proper equipment to be fighting these Serpens, so if we encounter any more on the road, we do *not* engage! We keep riding. They don't seem to be able to outrun horses and I didn't notice any of them carrying a bow, so we should be able to evade them. Understood?"

The group collectively replied, "Yes, Sergeant."

Colm nodded. "All right, let's move!"

They all spurred their horses into a fast gallop and continued up the road.

Kieran's adrenaline had now had time to dissipate, and he was all of the sudden overcome with grief at the realization that Donal, his closest friend, was gone. The image of a spear being rammed straight through Donal's neck kept replaying in his mind. Kieran was very thankful for the long ride to the southern outpost. It gave him the opportunity to let the tears flow.

The platoon arrived at the southern outpost two hours later. The outpost was nestled on a hill near the edge of a thin forest overlooking the plains to the south. The soldiers were still on edge and keeping a close eye on the forest and the tall grass, but they had not seen any further signs of Serpens since they had been attacked hours earlier.

Captain Martin was in charge of the southern patrols for the week's rotation, and he was alerted of the arrival of what remained of Kieran's platoon by the sentries. It was never good news to see a patrol return ahead of schedule, so he dropped everything he had been doing and met the platoon outside.

Sergeant Colm dismounted his horse and hurried over to Martin, giving a hasty salute as he walked. Martin immediately noticed that only half of the platoon was present, and his heart dropped. As soon as Colm had reached him, he said, "Tell me what's happened, Sergeant."

Colm gave his report of the events of the Serpen attack. Martin was surprisingly composed during the whole report. After Colm had finished, he stood there silently and surveyed the faces of the survivors.

Colm let the silence linger as long as he could stand, then finally asked, "What are your orders, Captain?"

Martin shifted his gaze to Colm and said, "Thank you, Sergeant." He turned to the remainder of the platoon and continued, "All of you go inside out of this heat and get some food and rest. You've earned it."

They all began to file through the gate. Colm started to walk toward the outpost entrance, but Martin put his hand on Colm's shoulder and said, "Not you."

Captain Martin was a forty-two-year-old experienced veteran of the Human army and was assigned to be the patrol captain of the southern outpost eleven years ago. Martin's experience and skills made him a superb captain, and he had the respect of every soldier under his command. This assignment was done out of an act of courtesy by the commander at that time. Martin had fought in many battles and served bravely for his entire career, and it was thought that assigning him to the southern region of Hume would provide him with a more peaceful service in his advanced years as a soldier. After all, the Serpens had never crossed their border, and the greater Orcovan threat lay to the north. This was supposed to be Martin's easy transition into retirement.

After all the men had entered the outpost, Martin stared out across the beautiful view of the plains of Hume. Colm was beginning to get annoyed by the captain's delay in responding.

He was about to ask him for orders again when Martin finally said, "I've never seen a Serpen in person, but what I *have* heard sounds like something straight out of a child's nightmare. Few who have the opportunity to see one live to tell the tale, and you and the rest of the survivors now know exactly why that is." He turned and looked at Colm. "You're certain you were nowhere near their border?"

Colm nodded, "Yes, sir. Not even close."

Martin continued, "Think carefully—did it look like they were after anything? Weapons? Food? Water?"

Colm hesitated, then said, "Not that I could tell, sir. But . . . it all happened so fast. I can't be certain."

Martin nodded and again looked out over the landscape before him. He continued, "We've always suspected our climate is simply too cold for them, and that's why they never leave Serpenta. After all, they are reptilian, and reptiles are cold-blooded." He shrugged. "It makes sense they would prefer the heat of the Serpentan Desert."

Martin shook his head turned his gaze to the ground in front of him. "This summer has been unusually warm, and I'd be lying if I said I hadn't considered the possibility of the Serpens getting a little more adventurous and traveling further north. Perhaps this is my fault for not insisting our patrols be more vigilant . . ."

He exhaled loudly and turned back to Sergeant Colm. "There will need to be a formal debriefing, but something of this significance must be done in Enlanor with individuals higher up than me. Given the danger of the present situation, I hate to lose what's left of your platoon, but you will all need to go to Enlanor to be debriefed. So, go inside and get some food and rest. Your platoon will leave for the capital in one hour. Keep them safe."

"Yes, Captain," replied Colm.

Martin put his hand on Colm's shoulder. "You did well today, Colm. You're dismissed."

"Thank you, sir." Colm turned and walked toward the gate of the outpost. Martin stayed outside overlooking the landscape, deep in thought. He was about the follow Colm inside when he noticed another platoon of soldiers galloping hastily up the road toward the outpost.

Martin shook his head and, under his breath said, "What now?"

When the second platoon arrived, the lieutenant practically fell off his horse in a panic. He ran over to Martin and exclaimed, "Captain! Dunsbury has been attacked!"

Just about the time Donal was investigating the tall grass in front of him and Kieran, a fifty-two-year-old man named Callum was tending to his crops nine miles to the west. It was exhausting work, but he much preferred running a homestead over active military service. Callum had served his mandatory five years and chose to build his home in the homestead community of Dunsbury to live a quiet, secluded life with his wife. That was over thirty years ago now, and he never looked back. The peaceful lifestyle of a homesteader suited him much better than that of a soldier.

Dunsbury began as just one homestead of a middle-aged couple seeking peace and seclusion, but more and more couples desiring that same seclusion in a like-minded community moved into the area. The homesteaders began to trade with one another and eventually developed their own microeconomy. They had little contact with the rest of Human society, which was exactly the way they liked it.

Callum took a break from tearing the ground with his rake and wiped the sweat from his brow with the sleeve of his dirt-stained tunic.

"What I wouldn't give for some shade right about now," he said aloud. His wife, Allanah, often chided him for talking to himself, but it was a habit he struggled to break. He looked over at a nearby tree and the shade it offered. He considered it for a moment but then shook his head said, "You can rest when you've finished, Callum."

He was about to continue his work when he noticed the cows in the pasture were acting very anxious, similar to the way they would act when a predator was nearby. He surveyed the area looking for signs of trouble, but he saw none. The grass of the fields gently waved in the wind, and all seemed quiet. Callum shrugged his shoulders and continued his raking when he suddenly heard a rustling in the shrubs behind him.

What was that? he thought. He started to turn and investigate the noise when he was slammed in the back by the weight of something very heavy behind him. He stumbled forward onto his hands and knees, struggling to breathe, for his breath had been knocked from his lungs.

He began to feel something wrap itself tightly around his legs and move upward and around his torso. He was incapable of moving, and he could feel it getting tighter with each passing second.

A large reptilian face worked its way into the right side of his peripheral vision and floated directly in front of his face. He saw two large yellow eyes with narrow, vertical pupils staring directly into his. Callum tried to scream, but he could feel the air being forced from his lungs as the constriction grew tighter. He felt a sharp, excruciating crack in one of his ribs. Then another. Then another. Searing pain shot through his chest. Callum could feel blood rushing to his head, and the pressure grew greater and greater. He had a throbbing headache, and his vision began slowly blur and darken. His mind became foggy, and he struggled to stay awake. As Callum's world faded away into darkness, the last thing he saw was more Serpens slithering through his field toward the village and those sinister yellow eyes still staring back into his.

5

SERGEANT COLM AND what was left of his platoon departed from the outpost with full bellies and feeling physically rejuvenated, but their emotional state was another matter entirely. They had all lost dear friends that day. These men spent more time together than with their own families, and over half of them were now gone.

The mood was extremely solemn as they rode northwest toward Enlanor. Colm wanted to say something to lift the men's spirits, but what could one say at a time like this? He resolved to keep silent and simply lead the group down the road.

Martin had sent another rider from the second platoon with them to give his account of what they found in what was left of Dunsbury.

Kieran loosely gripped the rei   ns and struggled to keep his mind on something, *anything* else, but he couldn't. Every time he looked out over what remained of the platoon, his eyes tore up.

The journey back to Enlanor was uneventful. They arrived at the city gates a little before sunset, and the news they were carrying was kept under wraps to prevent a city-wide panic.

The visiting council members from Elvenna and Dwarvonia were thankfully still in Enlanor, and King Aidan called for an emergency meeting. The council members wasted no time reporting for the meeting, for they knew that the situation must be dire for Aidan to call an emergency meeting.

The council members all promptly filed into the same chamber as they had earlier in the day, and Sergeant Colm was brought before them to give his testimony. Colm recounted the incident for the fifth time in the past day, and the council members stared in disbelief as he described everything that had happened. King Aidan and Commander Connor were the only members who had no reaction at all, but this was only due to the fact that they had already heard Colm's testimony.

The Dwarven commander spoke up, "How can this be? What would provoke the Serpens to leave Serpenta? This is unprecedented!"

Aidan nodded and said, "Indeed. And what's worse, it wasn't the only attack yesterday."

The room went silent as the council all stared at him in anticipation. He continued, "The entire population of Dunsbury, one of Hume's small villages in the south, were killed. Dunsbury is less than ten miles west of where Sergeant Colm's platoon was attacked."

The Dwarven King Oleg asked, "What was the population of the village?"

"Approximately thirty adults. Dunsbury was a small community of reclusive, middle-aged to elderly homesteaders."

Amrynn, the Elven King, said, "What do we know about the second attack?"

Commander Connor answered, "Very little. One of our patrols arrived on the scene after the attack was over. They found the strewn bodies of its inhabitants across the community. Some had spear wounds, others had been crushed to death. Oddly, the livestock all appeared untouched. Given the testimony of Sergeant Colm, this was obviously a Serpen attack."

Amrynn asked, "And these have been the only two sightings?"

"Correct," responded Connor.

Oleg spoke up again. "May we see a map of Hume with the locations of the attacks marked?"

"Of course," replied Aidan. He stood up from the table and walked to the chamber door. He opened the door and asked one of the guards outside to retrieve a map of Hume and bring it to the council chamber at once. As the guard left, Aidan returned to his seat and the discussion continued.

Dimitri, the Dwarven Commander, said, "Are we to suppose this is the answer to the riddle of the missing Human patrols you mentioned earlier, Connor?"

"I would say so, yes," replied Connor.

Dimitri continued, "Which means the Serpens have been in Hume for longer than just a few days . . ."

Connor and Aidan both nodded. They, too, had drawn the same conclusion.

Shaking his head, Oleg said, "But . . . the Serpens are very large and would stick out like a cow in a flock of sheep. How is it that no one has spotted them until now?"

Sergeant Colm cleared his throat and said, "If I may, my men and I came within a hundred feet of them out on the prairie and never saw them until they attacked. They're predators. Predators know how to hide."

Everyone in the council nodded in agreement.

Amrynn asked, "Do we have any theories regarding the Serpens' motive here? What reasons would they have to suddenly violate the Human border after ages of never leaving Serpenta? In fact, unless I'm mistaken, they have *never* come into Hume, correct?"

Aidan responded, "Not that our historical records indicate, no, but we have a couple of ideas as to their motive. Perhaps there are dwindling resources in Serpenta, forcing them to move further north? Another idea is that the unusually hot weather this summer is expanding the region in which their cold-blooded bodies can thrive, but this is all just conjecture."

Elven Commander Gildir asked, "Are you certain all other homes and villages are accounted for and safe?"

"As far as we know. Thankfully, the population is not as dense in the southern region of Hume," said Connor.

Aidan spoke up. "True, but one dead citizen of Hume is one too many." He paused for a moment, then stood up and continued, "The Serpens are in Hume. They're not only attacking soldiers, but civilians as well. The decision has already been made by myself and Connor to deploy three battalions to the southern region—"

There was a knock on the chamber door. Aidan motioned for Connor to go to the door and bring the map they had requested. Aidan continued, "As I was saying, three battalions have been deployed to the south to try to halt any further Serpen advances."

Connor unrolled the map of Hume onto the round table in front of the council members. Aidan pointed to two different locations on the map. "Here and here are the locations of yesterday's attacks." He then pointed to three other locations. "Here, here, and here are the locations we have sent our battalions."

Dwarven King Oleg said, "I will see to it that you have one of my Dwarven battalions at your disposal." Oleg turned to his commander. "Dimitri? You and Connor discuss the details of where they will be deployed." Dimitri nodded.

Elven King Amrynn then added, "And you shall have a battalion of Elvenna's warriors as well." He nodded at Gildir, his commander, and Gildir nodded back.

Aidan gave a slight nod and said, "Thank you, my friends. I hate the thought of my own people being killed, and I certainly don't enjoy the thought of yours being killed either. Let's hope the extra warriors won't be needed." Aidan turned to Connor and continued, "Do think there's any use in asking our Aquarian friends for aid as well?"

Connor snickered and replied, "*Friends?* Interesting choice of words . . . We can try, but I wouldn't expect much. They hardly even pay their taxes, so I doubt they'll send soldiers. I'll send out our ambassador to Aquaria tonight, and . . ." Connor shrugged. "Maybe we'll get lucky."

Aidan nodded and turned to the rest of the room. "Commanders? Work out the logistics. When you're finished, Connor and I will mount up and ride south."

Connor spoke up. "Forgive me, my king, but I'd rather you stayed here. I know you always prefer to ride out with your soldiers, but this situation is just too dangerous. We have no idea what we will encounter. The entire Serpentan army could be marching into Hume as we speak, for all we know."

"I appreciate your concern, but I insist on always being with my soldiers when they ride off to battle," said Aidan.

Connor replied, "We don't even know if there's a battle to ride off to yet. I'll go and lead them. I implore you, my king, stay here with the rest of the council. They need you here."

Aidan had a disgusted look on his face. "All right. Only because there is too much we don't know, I'll relent this time. But don't expect me to roll over so easily again!"

Connor smiled and turned to the other commanders. "Gentlemen? Shall we?"

Both nodded, and they left the chamber to begin their discussion of troop deployments.

Aidan turned to Kings Amrynn and Oleg. "Might I suggest that you all stay in Enlanor until this situation has been resolved? I fear the roads are too dangerous, plus we may require further sessions in the near future as this situation develops. Each of you are more than welcome in my palace."

Oleg laughed and said, "You put up such a fight about traveling to be with your troops, and then you try and convince each of us to stay here? That's a bit hypocritical, wouldn't you say?"

Both Aidan and Amrynn laughed. Being your quintessential Dwarf, Oleg was assertive and opinionated, but he was a good friend to them both.

Aiden replied, "I'm not concerned about my own safety nearly as much as yours. I would feel simply awful if something were to happen to any of you while in my province."

Each foreign council member bowed and accepted Aidan's gracious offer to stay in his palace.

The council meeting ended just as the sun had finished sinking below the horizon, and the sky above Enlanor was a beautiful canvas of orange and pink.

A flock of birds was resting on the top of the wall above the city gate. The gate suddenly began to lower, and the startled birds flew off at once.

Three riders, each with a platoon of mounted soldiers as escorts, burst out of the gate with great haste. The first group rode north toward Elvenna, the second east toward Dwarvonia, and the third southwest toward Aquaria.

6

THE NEWS OF a Serpen attack had naturally come as a shock to everyone in Hume. Until now, the Serpens hadn't been considered to be a threat unless you crossed the border into the Serpentan Desert, and there was never a need for that. The hot, arid environment alone was quite hostile, not to mention its dangerous inhabitants.

There was a lot of apprehension among the soldiers over the thought of going to war with Serpenta. None of them had ever fought a Serpen, but they had all heard the stories. Some of the stories were myth, some were factual, but the telling of these stories resulted in the Serpens having a terrifying reputation among the Humans. The Orcovans have a strong, efficient military, and no single province of the Andruvian Union could match the strength of the Orcovans alone. And though they were formidable adversaries, the soldiers at least knew how to fight them. Orcs were a foe they understood. The Serpens were something different entirely, and none of them knew what to expect.

The eyewitness accounts from what remained of Sergeant Colm's platoon were thoroughly examined, and the tactics the soldiers would be employing on the battlefield were adjusted accordingly. The plan was to ensure that every soldier was heavily armored to provide more protection from the Serpen spears, and archers were instructed to pack an extra quiver of arrows. None of the survivors from Colm's platoon had recalled seeing Serpen archers, and no arrow wounds were seen in the bodies from the Dunsbury attack. Furthermore, the Serpens used shields, but they weren't wearing any armor. Aidan and Connor determined the best way to fight this enemy was with ranged weapons and heavy armor.

The Serpens had experimented with different types of armor but found them to only limit their combat effectiveness. Serpens' bodies, like those of any snake, are very flexible, and their fighting style takes advantage of this mobility. Plate, scale, and leather armor severely restricted their body movement and did not allow them to utilize their biological advantages. Chainmail armor was flexible enough to not restrict their movement; however, it gave them much difficulty when trying to slither. The ventral surface of their bodies needed to be in contact with the ground to move quickly and efficiently, and chainmail prohibited that. They experimented with different prototypes but ultimately decided to not use armor at all and instead train their soldiers to be fast, agile fighters. Their defense centered around the use of a large tower shield, which they use very effectively due to their superior speed and reflexes.

～

Kieran stared at the ceiling of the barracks as he rested on his bunk. He was feeling mildly nauseous from just forcing down breakfast. He didn't have much of an appetite, but he hadn't eaten since breakfast on the morning of the Serpen ambush, so he had to eat *something*.

What remained of his platoon had been constantly bombarded by soldiers asking questions about the Serpen ambush since their arrival. Everyone seemed to be asking the same things: "What was it like?" "How fast are they?" "Did you spot any weaknesses?" Most were asking out of morbid curiosity, but some asked more so out of fear. They were visibly anxious about the likelihood of having to face these enemies and wanted as much information that they could get.

Kieran, Sergeant Colm, and the others tried to answer the questions as best as they could, but they honestly didn't have much to tell. The ambush only lasted a matter of seconds, and most of them barely even had enough time to draw their swords, let alone actually engage the enemy.

Kieran wanted to catch up on his sleep before their new orders came through, but sleep eluded him. The events of the ambush and the anticipation of what would come next kept running through his mind.

Colm walked into the entrance of the barracks and began walking toward Kieran and the others, and they all shuffled to their feet and awaited the news.

Colm looked at his men and said, "Well, for the time being we've been reassigned to B company under the command of Captain Finnian of the northern patrol."

Several of the men exchanged knowing looks. Finnian's reputation preceded him. He was young, but his swordsman skills were well known among the patrol. He rarely ever lost a sparring match, and no one had ever beaten him twice. Furthermore, he was clearly a natural leader and earned the respect of every man under his command.

Colm gave an audible sigh, then continued, "Unfortunately, B company is being deployed later today. They're sending us south to an area just outside of Dunsbury. So, if any of you have family in Enlanor, go see them now."

The whole group was silent. They had all of course heard the news of the Dunsbury attack, and none of them relished the thought of meeting the Serpens on the battlefield a second time. They were secretly hoping that perhaps they'd be given leave to recuperate after their ordeal, but they figured the chances were remote.

Kieran's family lived far away, so he simply laid back down on his bunk and shut his eyes. He tried his best to shut his mind off and fall asleep, but he couldn't stop his mind from imagining what lay ahead.

~

Finnian awoke early to start the morning patrol with his platoon in the areas surrounding Enlanor. The patrols during the city rotation did not cover as much ground as the outpost rotations; therefore the route was able to be finished in a much shorter amount of time. Finnian spent most of the patrol planning the day's schedule in his head. He intended to spend the afternoon with Reagan and then meet the rest of the royal family at the palace for dinner.

His platoon finished the patrol by late morning, and Finnian was anxious to report to Major Brady so he could be released for the remainder of the day. Finnian was hitching his horse by the barracks when he saw Brady standing near the entrance as if he had been waiting for him. Finnian thought it odd but did not think any more of it.

He approached Brady and began to give his report when the major abruptly held up his hand, a gesture instructing Finnian to stop.

"Were there any incidents?" asked Brady.

"No, sir," answered Finnian.

Brady continued, "Fine. The rest of the patrol captains on their city rotation are waiting in the briefing hall. I need to speak to all of you *now*." Brady stepped aside and motioned with his arm for Finnian to enter the building.

Finnian had a sick feeling in his stomach. *Something's happened*, he thought.

He walked into the briefing hall and saw the rest of the patrol captains waiting. Everyone appeared on edge, for they all suspected that something bad had occurred for the major to call a meeting with them like this. Finnian sat in the nearest seat and waited for Brady to start the briefing.

Brady stood at the front of the hall and said, "The reason I've gathered you all here is to update you on the situation as we currently know it. Yesterday, one of the southern patrol platoons was attacked by a group of Serpens. The eyewitness accounts conflict a little, but the general consensus is that there were seven or eight Serpens total." Brady paused, then continued, "Gentlemen, over half of the platoon was killed, and the other half barely escaped with their lives." He paused a second time to give the captains a moment to digest this information. There were immediate rumblings and hushed exclamations of shock among the audience.

After the rumblings had died down, Brady continued. "There was also a second incident yesterday . . ."

The group listened intently as they waited for even more bad news. They were almost wincing in pain as the suspense built.

Brady continued, "Serpens attacked the homestead community of Dunsbury and left no survivors." There were even more exclamations of shock in the room. "You are to remain on standby and await further orders. I'm sorry, Captains. I know you all just started your city rotation and were looking forward to spending time with your families, but it looks as though we will all be deployed here shortly. There is nothing more I know at this time, so please, no questions. Now go and update your men on the situation."

The captains began filing out of the room, having hushed conversations with one another. Some were almost excited at the chance to fight a new foe, especially one as fearsome as the Serpens. Others were more apprehensive about what this turn of events could possibly mean.

Finnian didn't know what to think. Both soldiers and civilians have been killed. Did this mean they were at now war with the mysterious, reclusive race that has perplexed Andruvians for ages? There were many questions, but no answers.

It didn't take long for them to receive their orders. Three Human battalions were being deployed to the south to protect the southern region of Hume. Finnian's battalion would be dispatched to a location that was just north of Dunsbury, and they were to hold that position. They were also notified that a battalion of Elves and a battalion of Dwarves would also be rendezvousing with them as soon as they were able.

The answer to Finnian's question seemed to have been answered—a deployment of five battalions from all three members of the Andruvian Union certainly seemed to indicate that they were going to war . . .

Finnian found an opportunity to leave the barracks and visit Reagan at the palace. He had no idea how long he would be deployed, and he had to see her before he left. He walked into the palace entrance and asked the first servant he saw where he could find Reagan. As usual, she was in the library.

Finnian walked in and saw her sitting in the same spot as last night. A slight feeling of dread came over him as he saw her sitting there. He had looked forward to spending time with her all week, and now he had to leave again. But Finnian clenched his jaw and shook off those feelings of doubt. He was a soldier, a servant of Hume.

Reagan looked at Finnian, and her face lit up. "Finnian! I thought you said you wouldn't be released until later this afternoon?"

Finnian sat down next to her, took ahold of her hand, and said, "There's been a change of plans. There were two attacks down near the southern border, and they're deploying us to go check things out." He intentionally did not mention the fact that the attackers were Serpens, for their terrifying reputation was well known to all.

"Oh . . .," Reagan replied. There was visible disappointment on her face. "Well, do you have any idea how long you'll be gone?"

Finnian shook his head. "No."

Reagan volunteered a little smile and shrugged. "Duty calls. I'll be here when you get back."

Finnian gave her a hug and said, "Thank you. We're leaving soon, so I should go and prepare."

Reagan smiled and said, "Good-bye, Finnian. Be safe."

Finnian nodded. He didn't want to leave so abruptly, but he didn't know what else to say. He finally stood up and began walking out of the library.

As he left, Reagan struggled to keep the smile on her face. She worried about Finnian every time he left the city on patrol. She knew that this was no ordinary precaution if soldiers were being deployed. Deployment was typically only necessary when there was a very real possibility of a battle. Her smile faded as soon as he left, and tears began rolling down her face.

～

The sunlight cascaded through the leaves on the trees as Finnian and the rest of the battalion rode south toward their assigned destination. He and his closest friend, Lieutenant Galen, rode side by side along the road as the battalion made its way further south. The company commanded by Finnian was leading the battalion down the road. If they were going to encounter resistance, they would likely be the first ones to make contact.

"What do you think is going on?" asked Galen. "Why do you think they invaded all of the sudden?"

Finnian replied, "We don't have any evidence this is an invasion. For all we know, this could just be a group of rogue Serpens."

"And if it's not?" replied Galen.

Finnian shook his head. "I don't know . . . I just don't want us to get ourselves into the middle of another war. With the help of the Elves and Dwarves, we can handle the Orcs, but I don't know if we can fight *two* enemies."

Galen could hear the concern in Finnian's voice, so he decided to change the subject. "So, we're going to rendezvous with a battalion of Elves?"

Finnian nodded. "That's the plan. We are the furthest west of the three deployed battalions. The Elves are going to meet up with us, and the Dwarves are going to meet the easternmost battalion. Then we are supposed to hold our positions and await further orders. They are sending out patrols all over the southern region looking for any more signs of the Serpens. If they're still here, we'll find them."

Finnian glanced ahead, then behind. He looked at Galen and said, "The company is getting a little too spread out. Ride up ahead and tell your platoon to slow their pace. I'll drop back and try to quicken the rear platoon."

Galen nodded and said, "I'm on it."

Galen quickened his horse's gallop and rode ahead, and Finnian turned his horse around and galloped toward the rear and rode up to Lieutenant Sean, the officer commanding the rear platoon.

"Sean," said Finnian, "Your platoon is lagging behind. Make sure you keep pace with the rest of the company."

Sean briefly looked out over his platoon and nodded in agreement. "Yes, sir," he replied.

Finnian began riding back to the front when he spotted Sergeant Colm.

Ah, these must be the new guys, he thought. Things had been so hectic that he hadn't yet had the chance to introduce himself, so he rode over to Colm.

Colm spotted him, gave a salute, and said, "Captain. Sergeant Colm, F company, first platoon."

Finnian nodded back and said, "Nice to meet you, Colm. It's good to have you with us."

"Thank you, sir," replied Colm.

Finnian surveyed the unfamiliar faces of Colm's platoon, and his gaze met with Kieran's. Finnian closed the distance between them, and Kieran said, "Private Kieran, sir."

Finnian gave a single nod and said, "Where are you from, Kieran?"

Kieran thought it was refreshing to be asked a question not related to the Serpen ambush. "Born and raised in Cliften, sir," he replied.

Finnian smiled and said, "Ah! I've been there! I ride by Cliften on my patrol route. Lieutenant Galen and I have gone to a pub there called the Yellow Oak."

Kieran's eyes got wide and he said, "That's my family's pub! I worked there before going to the academy!"

Finnian laughed. "No kidding! Wow . . . Well, give my compliments to your family the next time you see them!"

"Yes, sir!" replied Kieran.

The road the battalion was following began to cut through a dense forest. Dunsbury was located several miles south of the other side of this forest, and they were getting close to their assigned location.

Finnian turned to another soldier riding next to Kieran and began to say, "How about you? Where are you fr—"

Finnian cut off midsentence. There was a commotion and yelling at the front! He tightly clutched the reins and sprinted his horse toward the front as quickly as he could.

7

GALEN GALLOPED UP to the lead platoon that was under his direct command. The battalion was several miles northwest of Dunsbury and was currently getting bottlenecked on a narrow road through a forest. Galen spotted one of his sergeants and began to gallop alongside him.

"Sergeant, we need to slow the pace a little. The rear platoon is lagging behind."

The sergeant nodded and said, "Yes, sir." He quickened the pace of his horse to reach the soldiers at the very front and began relaying the orders.

Galen began to survey his surroundings and started to feel uneasy. Cutting through this forest on a narrower road would be a perfect place for an ambush. Unfortunately, it was also the quickest route to their destination, and there was no other direct route through the forest.

Galen shook his head and rode up alongside his sergeant again. He was still relaying the orders as Galen reached him and said, "Keep your eyes on the forest. We're in a really bad spot right now."

The sergeant nodded in agreement, and Galen turned his horse around and started making his way back toward Finnian. As he was riding back down the line, a flood of arrows from the forest suddenly showered the Humans. There was screaming and yelling as men fell from their hoses onto the ground. The arrows seemed to be coming from every direction, and immediately everything was complete chaos.

Galen raised his shield up to protect himself in at least one direction and tried to survey the situation and formulate a plan. He opened his mouth to start yelling orders when his horse suddenly jumped and whined loudly. He looked down and saw a tan wooden arrow protruding from the left side of his horse's neck. The horse's legs started to buckle. Galen slid his left foot out of the stirrup, slung his leg over the horse's back, and jumped to the ground as quickly as he could. After landing, he immediately brought up his shield and readied his spear.

Finnian was racing to the front when he realized what was happening. There were archers in the forest on both sides of the road firing into the soldiers. They were caught in a crossfire!

So much for the Serpens not having archers . . . We need to get off this road! We need cover from the arrows! he thought.

Their only option was to go into the forest, but he knew the enemy would be waiting for them. *Very clever*, he thought, *but we don't have a choice.*

Finnian began to yell, "Into the forest! Into the forest! Keep shields at the ready!" The order was relayed throughout the company, and the men began to run for the cover of the trees.

It didn't take long for Colm's men to be fired upon after Finnian began racing to the front. They were engulfed with arrows from both sides of the dense forest, and men and horses were screaming.

An arrow glanced off Kieran's chest plate and continued on its trajectory. It hadn't been a direct hit. Every instinct in Kieran's body told him to get low to the ground.

He freed his feet from the stirrups and clumsily dove off his horse and onto the ground. He lifted his head off the ground and looked to his left—nothing but dense forest. He couldn't even see the archers. He looked to his right—he was suddenly staring directly into the lifeless face of Sergeant Colm. Like Kieran, an arrow had glanced off his chest plate as well, but he was less fortunate. The arrow glanced directly upward and lodged deeply underneath his jaw. Colm was dead.

Kieran quickly turned his head away and saw that soldiers were pouring into the forest with their swords or spears drawn and their shields ready. He brought himself to a kneeling position, drew his sword, and followed his fellow soldiers into the forest. As they did, there was suddenly a loud, terrifying howl coming from the forest on all sides of them. It was a sound none of them had ever heard before, and it made the hair on the back of their necks stand up.

Finnian was right. The Serpens were expecting them to run for cover into the forest. Hundreds of Serpen warriors were lying flat against the ground using bushes and shrubs for concealment as their archers fired volley after volley into the huddled mass of soldiers. As soon as the Humans began to enter the forest, the arrows abruptly stopped. The low-lying Serpen warriors were waiting for the perfect moment to spring into action.

The news of the attack had now reached the entire battalion, which was spread out over a distance of half a mile. The remaining companies rode furiously toward the front to join the fight. Riders were sent to the other battalions to bring word of the attack.

The first of the soldiers flooded into the dense forest with shields and weapons ready. The archers inched their way in with arrows knocked, waiting for an opportunity to draw and release.

In an instant, the hidden Serpen warriors jolted forward, thrusting their spears. The sound of Serpen spears crashing into Human shields echoed throughout the forest. The spears sank firmly into the shields, knocking the soldiers off balance, some even off their feet.

Finnian ran into the forest presenting his shield, fully expecting to be hit by a spear. He was not disappointed. Finnian didn't even have time to react before a spear slammed into his shield.

He caught a glimpse of the creature in front of him, and it sent a shiver down his spine. These creatures were massive! A scaly brown figure balanced its torso off the ground at a height of eight feet. Its back was a darker shade of brown, and its belly and chest were a lighter tan color. It held a large rectangular shield with its left arm and wielded a long, heavy spear with its right. Finnian had heard about their size and had seen artists' depictions of their appearance, but neither had prepared him for the creature that now stood in front of him. The manner in which its body bent and writhed looked so alien to Finnian. Simply put, the Serpens were terrifying.

The Serpen's spear strike wasn't a direct hit, and the tip glanced off the side of Finnian's shield. Trying to track the Serpens when striking was next to impossible. They almost were too fast for Human eyes to follow. Before he hardly had a chance to recover from the first strike, the Serpen jolted another spear thrust forward.

Finnian immediately reacted after feeling the impact of the spear. He used his shield to slam the Serpen's spear aside and thrust his own spear toward the Serpen. The Serpen easily blocked the spear thrust with his own shield and drew back, preparing for another strike.

This won't work. I have to let him get closer . . . thought Finnian.

Just then, he had an idea. He dropped his spear, drew his sword, and adjusted his grip on his shield. Finnian and his reptilian foe stared each other in the eyes until he finally screamed, *"Do it!"*

The Serpen let out a sinister hiss and darted forward. Finnian braced himself for the impact. He felt a massive slam into his shield and was knocked slightly off-balance, but he recovered quickly. He pulled his shield close to his body, and with as much speed as he could muster, rolled directly toward the Serpen, whose torso was now only eight feet away from him.

Keeping his shield between him and the Serpen, he came out of the roll and immediately thrust his sword upward with all the strength his arm possessed. He felt the steel sink into soft flesh, and the Serpen let out a bloodcurdling screech like nothing Finnian had ever heard before. He looked up and saw that his sword was lodged deep within the Serpen's body at roughly the location where the Human abdomen would be.

He adjusted his grip on his sword and sliced it downward, producing a massive, gaping wound in the Serpen's body. Blood and viscera poured out of the wound, and the Serpen writhed and twisted on the ground until its body finally relaxed and rested motionless on the ground.

Finnian knelt on the ground, panting from exhaustion. Sweat dripped into his eyes, and he rubbed them with the back of his gloved hands. Not many could have successfully completed the somewhat foolish move Finnian just performed. It wasn't practical, and it left him very open to a counterattack during the roll. As he knelt on the ground, he decided that though it was successful this time, it would eventually get him killed. He would need a new tactic. He stood to his feet, sheathed his sword, picked up his spear, and looked around him.

Everything was pandemonium. There were screams and clashing of steel. Bodies were strewn all over the forest floor, and he couldn't help but notice that very few of them were Serpen bodies. The Serpens they had killed were mostly brought down by the archers. The Human casualties were too high.

The remainder of the battalion had arrived and joined the fight, but the difference they made was negligible. The other two battalions were not far off, but Finnian had to face the hard reality that this was a fight they couldn't win. They needed to get out of this forest and fight the Serpens in an open field. There they could *possibly* be more effective by utilizing their archers and staying in formation. The Serpens were winning the one-on-one fight.

Finnian's eyes darted back and forth. *Where's Galen?* he thought.

Galen was doing all he could to lead his men, but there was no structure to this fight. There were no battle lines. The forest was too dense, and it had devolved into a massive free-for-all. Galen had lost his spear and had his sword drawn. His shield was almost destroyed from blocking repeated spear thrusts. The Serpens were just too fast.

He saw a Serpen warrior distracted by a group of five soldiers it was fighting, and he sprinted toward it with his sword ready. The Serpen hardly even recognized Galen's approach before he thrust his sword into its body, the bloody steel emerging out the other side. The Serpen howled in pain, and the other soldiers it had been fighting dealt the final blows to end its life. Feeling accomplished, Galen tried to withdraw his sword from its carcass, but the blade was stuck. He turned and looked deeper into the forest and saw another Serpen quickly slithering toward him, spear at the ready. Galen barely had enough time to shift into a defensive stance before the Serpen struck.

Finnian made his way through the brawl and finally spotted Galen. He was trying to withdraw his sword from the body of a dead Serpen warrior. Finnian started running toward him but then noticed another Serpen approaching Galen.

Galen presented his shield and waited for the strike. The Serpen shot forward, but instead of thrusting its spear, it bashed its shield into Galen's. Galen's already damaged shield broke into two pieces and he was thrown to the ground from the impact. The Serpen raised its spear and stabbed it toward Galen's neck, an area not as well protected by his armor. Galen swung what was left of his broken shield up to block the spear thrust and deflected it just in time. The Serpen bent down, grabbed Galen's broken shield, and pushed it aside. Using its other hand, it grabbed Galen's helmet, ripped the leather strap holding it in place, and slid it off his head. Galen laid there and solemnly stared at the Serpen. The two met eyes, and the Serpen let out a snarl. Galen was beaten. He was pinned to the ground and defenseless. He met the Serpen's gaze and bravely accepted when he knew was coming next. The Serpen lifted Galen's helmet upward toward the sky, then strongly swung it down onto his unprotected head.

Finnian watched the whole scene play out as he futilely tried to reach Galen in time. He watched the Serpen raise Galen's helmet and swing it down.

He screamed, "*Galen!*" as he rushed the Serpen and cut its right shoulder deeply with a downward strike of his sword. With a swift, continuous motion, he then bashed it in the head with his shield, and the Serpen staggered. It tried to recover, but Finnian had already begun a second swing of his sword. He horizontally sliced its exposed throat open, and bright red blood spilled out of the Serpen's neck as it tried to yell, but no sound came. It stumbled backward to the ground, grasping at its throat with its one good arm as it bled out.

Finnian looked down at the motionless body of his friend, but he had to quickly look away. There was no doubt. Galen was dead. He took a deep breath and tried to focus on the battle. Now was not the time for mourning.

~

In a sense, there were two battles occurring—one on each side of the road that ran through the forest. Finnian and Galen had entered the forest on the left side of the road, and the battle on the other side was not favoring the Humans any better.

More and more soldiers were pouring into both sides of the forest as the remaining battalions arrived on the scene, anxious for battle. Though the Serpens were outnumbered, the location of the battle gave them the advantage, which is precisely why they chose it. The forest was too dense to allow the Humans to fight in formation or have any reasonable visibility. Traveling on the long, narrow path of the road stretched the battalions too thin, and the tree-cluttered battleground of the forest isolated them enough to limit their advantage of having superior numbers.

~

The gruesome fight raged on. Kieran had stayed with a group of soldiers from his fellow platoon. They inched deeper and deeper into the forest while trying to maintain a semicircle of shields for protection. There were three archers in the center of the semicircle that would attempt to fire when there was an opportunity, but the close-quarters combat in the forest rarely presented one.

Kieran yelled out to the group, "What's the plan here!"

One of the soldiers replied, "Not die, that's the plan!"

Kieran responded, "We have to find an officer! We need orders!"

There was a consensus among the group, and they stopped advancing deeper into the forest and began moving parallel to the road . . . or at least what they thought was parallel. Their sense of direction in the forest amid the confusion of the battle was limited.

They were moving closer and closer toward the sounds of fighting when a Serpen suddenly burst forward from behind a tangle of shrubs and trees. It had been watching them and waited for the opportune time to strike.

It struck from the unprotected flank of the semicircle and buried the head of its spear into the base of an archer's neck. The archer toppled to the ground without making a sound, and the Serpen recoiled back to prepare for another strike.

The whole group of soldiers spun toward the Serpen with their shields raised, each of them trying their best to not step on the body of their fallen comrade.

The Serpen and the soldiers stared each other down, each waiting for the other to make the next move. Kieran's heart was almost beating out of his chest. The rush of adrenaline almost made him dizzy.

The Serpen let out a small hiss and was poising itself for another strike when suddenly an arrow lodged in its thorax, just beneath its left armpit. It let out an awful howl and retreated deeper into the forest while holding the arrow lodged in its ribs.

The men quickly looked to find the source of the arrow, and they saw a Human archer stringing another arrow and running toward the group.

"Nice shot!" said Kieran as the archer reached the group.

The archer hardly even acknowledged the compliment and simply asked, "Got room for one more?"

One of the soldiers replied, "The more the better!"

The archer was only a private like the rest of the soldiers in the group, and he asked, "Do we have any orders? What are we supposed to be doing? Are we fighting, are we retreating . . . ?"

Kieran shook his head. "We don't know either. We're trying to find an officer somewhere in this mess."

The archer nodded, and the group continued to slowly advance toward the sound of fighting.

Finnian had tried his best to keep his soldiers together as much as possible. There was strength in numbers when fighting these ruthless, agile foes. The surviving Humans all began adopting similar tactics to Kieran's group, forming either semicircles or complete circles of shield walls.

Suddenly, there was a loud blast of a horn in the distance. The horn had a high-pitched, warbling quality to it. Finnian heard it and said, "I know that horn . . . that's an Elven horn!"

The battalion of Elves had arrived. They weren't far from the forest when the riders carrying the message of the attack met them, and they raced to the battle as quickly as they were able.

Though they are physically weaker, Elves are faster, more agile, and have better coordination, dexterity, and reflexes than Humans. Their preferred melee weapons are two sabers which they would dual wield.

Dual-wielding swords was not practical for any other race in Andruvia because they lacked the coordination, speed, and reaction time necessary to use them effectively. Precise manipulation of two swords at once, each performing a different task, was only possible for the Elves.

Like the Serpens, the Elves developed their fighting style based upon their biological advantages. They sometimes utilized archery in combat, but only when necessary. Their weaker upper body strength limits the amount of draw weight an Elf can pull, resulting in less arrow penetration, especially when the target is armored. The Elves experimented with crossbows; however, the archers felt overencumbered carrying the awkward apparatus as opposed to the lighter recurve war bow.

~

The Elven battalion wasted no time engaging the Serpens. They split their numbers in half and charged straight into both sides of the forest with gusto, ready to test their mettle with this new enemy. Though the opportunity didn't occur very often, Finnian had always enjoyed fighting alongside these nimble warriors.

Just after hearing the Elves sound their horn, a Serpen warrior emerged from a cluster of pine trees seconds in front of Finnian. The two stared each other down, studying one another and waiting for the opportune time to strike. Finnian kept his battered shield raised to just below his chin so he could protect his torso but not obstruct his view. His sword was concealed behind the shield, but he kept it pointed directly at the Serpen, ready to be jabbed forward at a moment's notice.

The Serpen struck forward a distance of twenty feet, and Finnian just barely moved his shield in the way of the sharp spear thrust toward his head. The impact made his shield recoil and slam into his helmet, but he was not hurt.

Just then, an Elven warrior sprinted past him on the left toward the Serpen. As the Serpen was raising his shield with the intention of bashing Finnian, the Elf used a forehand slash with the saber in his right hand across the Serpen's chest. The Elf used the momentum of the saber swing and continued spinning his body around, bending at the knees as he did so. The Elf delivered another slash with his left saber in the Serpen's abdomen. The Serpen hissed in pain as it tried to recover, and it was abruptly silenced as the Elf stood back up and thrust his right saber into its open mouth. The whole maneuver only took a matter of seconds and would have impressed even the finest Human swordsman.

The Elf turned around and faced Finnian. Finnian gave him a brief nod, and the expression was understood.

The Elf returned the nod and then said, "Our orders are to get everyone out of the forest and retreat north up the road to regroup." The Elf noticed Finnian's insignia etched into the shoulders of his armor. "Where are the rest of your men, Captain?"

Finnian shrugged his shoulders and replied, "Everywhere. We were ambushed on the road and most of us got split up in the forest. But I agree, we need to get out of this forest. Let's get to work."

The Elf nodded and followed Finnian deeper into the forest to start passing along the retreat orders to everyone they could find.

~

The aid of the Elves in the forest battle was sorely needed; however, it was proving to be costly for the Elves. The offensive capabilities of the Elves wielding dual sabers were not without its trade-off: fewer defensive capabilities. The Elvish fighting style had primarily been tailored to fighting the Orcovans, and the speed and distanced striking capabilities of the Serpens made the lack of a shield very costly for them. Most Elves did carry bucklers as part of their loadout, but they didn't offer enough coverage for the Elves to defend against the Serpen spear strikes. For every Serpen the Elven warriors killed, twice as many were unable to evade the Serpens' lightning-fast attacks, costing them their lives.

Finnian was losing stamina. The midday heat was almost unbearable in his hot armor. He had been fighting almost constantly with no time for rest, and he could feel the strength being sapped from his muscles with every swing of his sword. Had it not been for his new Eleven friend, he likely would have already fallen. Finnian heard the sound of another horn. This horn projected a flat tone with more bass, and he instantly recognized this sound as well. *Dwarves!* he thought.

The Dwarves are impressively strong for their small stature. They are vigorous melee fighters with a low center of mass, making them difficult to throw off balance or knock over. Even so, the short reach of their arms put them at a significant disadvantage in combat. The Dwarves therefore prefer weapons that extend their reach. Their preferred primary weapon is a halberd, which consists of an axe blade topped with a spike mounted on a six-foot wooden shaft. The wielder of a halberd can get a lot of leverage when swinging, thus adding to the already powerful swing a Dwarf possesses. As a secondary weapon, the Dwarves carry an arming sword on their hip and a shield slung over their back. Dwarven tactics revolved around power and protection rather than speed and grace.

Like the Elves, Dwarves have a natural disadvantage when it comes to archery. Though they possess the strength to pull a heavy draw weight, their arms are too short to pull a full-sized war bow to full draw. Therefore, Dwarven archers prefer crossbows. Unlike the Elves, they have no qualms with carrying the bigger, heavier weapon and are able to reload it with a fair amount of ease due to their short, strong arms.

After entering the battle, the Dwarves quickly realized they would need to use their shields along with the halberd. They needed protection from the Serpens' deadly spear strikes, and they didn't have the speed and agility of the Elves to try to evade them.

After adjusting their tactics to adapt to this new enemy, the Dwarves put up a formidable fight against the Serpens. Because they are not easily knocked off balance and are so heavily armored, they were able to withstand the Serpens' strikes with more ease and bide their time to wait for an opening to counterattack.

Finnian and his Elven companion came upon a skirmish between a Serpen and a Human and a Dwarf. The Serpen struck at the Human, slamming him with its shield. The soldier fell to the ground, and the Serpen towered over him, raising its spear, preparing to stab it downward onto the soldier. At the same moment, the Dwarf swung his halberd around at the Serpen's head. The Serpen quickly brought his shield up and blocked the Dwarf's swing, and the axe head embedded deeply within the shield. While the Serpen was distracted, the Human, still holding his sword, thrust it toward the body of the Serpen.

The sword connected with its target and pierced into the reptile's soft abdomen. The Serpen grunted and recoiled, pulling the sword out of its abdomen. The wound was not a fatal one, but Finnian thought the Serpen would be stunned enough for them to take advantage of.

He and the Elf rushed in readying their swords. The Serpen dropped its shield with the halberd still firmly lodged in it and turned its head, watching the Human and the Elf sprint toward it. It tried to compose itself to retreat when the Dwarf drew his sword and stabbed it directly into its chest cavity, killing it almost instantly. Finnian and the Elf slowed their pace to a jog and approached the other Human and Dwarf.

Finnian said, "Nicely done. Start making your way out of the forest and retreat north back up the road. We are supposed to regroup there."

The Dwarf nodded and replied, "Yes, we have the same orders." The Human and the Dwarf jogged off through the forest toward the road.

Finnian watched the two of them disappear into the thicket, when he suddenly felt something slam into his left side. He was thrown straight to the ground by the impact. Finnian looked around to see what had hit him, and he saw a Serpen hovering above him, with the tip of its spear stuck into the side of the chest plate of his armor. The Serpen was pinning him to the ground, and he was unable to move.

At the same time Finnian was hit, his Elven companion was hit by a spear from a second Serpen, but his companion wasn't as fortunate. The Serpen's spear plunged deeply into the joint between the armor on his left shoulder and his chest plate.

The Elf sunk to the ground as the strength left his legs, and he folded over onto the ground. The Serpen removed his spear from the Elf's body and waited for the other to finish off Finnian.

The Serpen hovering over him raised its shield above its head, ready to slam the edge down into Finnian's exposed face, but just then, there was a snarl from behind the attacker.

The Serpen lowered the shield and looked at a third Serpen that had just emerged on the scene. Finnian noticed this third Serpen was wearing a decorative silver band around its neck. It let out a series of hisses and snarls, and the other two Serpens let out a single hiss in response.

It bent down and pinned Finnian's sword-wielding arm to the ground using its shield and ripped the sword out of his hand using its other arm. It brought its long tail around and coiled it around Finnian, totally immobilizing his limbs. The second Serpen approached with ropes and a large sack and bound Finnian's hands and feet. His mouth was then gagged, and he was thrown into the large sack.

8

SHORTLY AFTER THE Dwarves arrived, the Serpens started to retreat. The surviving Union soldiers were able to find their way out of the forest and regroup to the north to prepare for the possibility of a second attack, as well as start tallying their losses. The casualty estimate was horrifying. Every Human battalion had at least one quarter of their forces either dead or missing.

The details of the battle were reported to Connor, who had arrived from Enlanor at roughly the same time as the Dwarves. Throughout the report, he simply stared at his feet, shaking his head. Outwardly he appeared calm, but on the inside, he was fuming.

After the report was finished, Connor said, "They baited us. They attacked Dunsbury and one of our patrols to draw us out, face us on their own terms at the location of their choice." He turned to the Elven and the Dwarven officers who were present for the report and said, "If it weren't for each of your battalions, many more of my men would have been killed. Thank you."

They nodded in unison. Motioning to the Elf, the Dwarf said, "I don't want to speak for you, but I suggest we send word to our kings in Enlanor to request more soldiers immediately."

"I couldn't agree more," replied the Elf. "They may have retreated, but I hardly doubt we have seen the last of them."

"Their strategy was brilliant," said Connor. "Lure us out into the wilderness, ambush us while we are bottlenecked by the forest, and let us scatter into the forest out of formation and pick us off, one by one." He paused, took a deep breath, then continued, "We need to evacuate all the southern towns in Hume and bring the people to Enlanor, and we need to bring reinforcements and push south to protect our border. I'll report back to the council and update them at once. I can't imagine they would disagree, but I will return as quickly as I can with the official orders." Connor turned to his second in command and said, "Position what's left of our battalions out of archery range of the tree line and be ready for another attack."

"Absolutely," his officer replied.

Connor patted him on the shoulder and began preparing for the trip back to Enlanor.

~

Major Brady had a similar reaction to Commander Connor as the casualty reports came in. Too many of his men were dead. Furthermore, a lot of the officers were either dead or missing. Among the names of the missing was Captain Finnian.

As soon as he heard Finnian's name, he thought to himself, *Oh no . . .* He saw Connor in the distance and made his way over to him.

He approached Connor and said, "I'm sorry to bother you, Commander, but I know you were returning to Enlanor, and I have some news I'm sure the king will want to know."

Connor gave a slight nod, and Brady continued, "Captain Finnian is among the missing. I know he and the royal family are close. We haven't found his body yet, but we are still searching."

Connor let out a long sigh. He was familiar with Finnian. Not only did he have a sterling reputation as a soldier, he knew very well how much he meant to the king and the rest of his family. "Thank you, Major," Connor replied.

~

Kieran rested on his back in the grass and stared at the clear blue sky. There was not a cloud to be seen, and had it not been for the current circumstances, it was a beautiful day. His helmet lay on the grass beside him. He had been sweating profusely, and his hair was matted to his head. He and what was left of his platoon, which was now only several men, had just arrived at the rendezvous point and were awaiting further orders. Frankly, none of them really cared at this point. Those who made it out did so purely by luck. They had been face-to-face with the Serpens on two different occasions now, and each of them inwardly decided that there was little they could do to fight them. Should the fighting continue, as it was sure to do, they knew that eventually each one of them would fall. Donal was dead. Colm was dead. There was barely anyone left of their platoon. The Serpens were simply too deadly.

Another soldier sauntered over and sat down next to Kieran and the others. He stared at the grass in front of him for a moment, then addressed the group, saying, "Captain Finnian is missing."

The group all glanced in his direction, then at each other. For a long while, no one spoke. Eventually, one of them stood up, faced the tree line off in the distance, and growled, "When are these lizards going to show up and finally get this over with!"

He ripped off his helmet and spiked it to the ground. Kieran stood up and grabbed him by the arms, saying, "Hey! Take it easy! Take some deep breaths!"

He ripped his arms free and said, "I'm fine! Don't touch me!" He strode off away from the group, grumbling under his breath as they watched him leave. They all turned to one another and shared a weary look. They all felt the same way.

Kieran laid back down on the grass and continued staring up at the beautiful blue sky. He thought to himself, *If Finnian is no match for them, what chances do the rest of us have?*

~

Connor arrived in Enlanor and relayed the battle report to the council. Connor's report was met with sighs, shaking heads, and looks of shock.

After he was finished, Aidan said, "And so Hume is officially at war with Serpenta." He brought his hands to his face and rubbed his eyes.

Dwarven King Oleg slammed his fist onto the table. "No! The *Andruvian Union* is at war with Serpenta! Our soldiers died out there too! You have our full support! We'll beat these snakes back, just like we have with the Orcs!"

Oleg looked to the Elven King Amrynn for confirmation, and Amrynn said, "Absolutely, Aidan. I may not be as . . . *energetic* as Oleg, but I can assure you Hume will face no enemy alone."

With a slight smile, Aidan nodded and said, "All of Hume thanks you, my friends. It looks like we'll need all the help we can get." Aidan drew a deep breath and let it out slowly. He turned to Connor. "Do we have any new information as to why they are doing this?"

Connor shook his head. "No, nothing. But I recommend we evacuate all the southern communities and bring them here, and we need to send more soldiers to reinforce what's left of our battalions. We need to keep pushing south and secure our border."

Aidan nodded and said, "I agree. Connor, make the arrangements." He turned to Oleg and Amrynn. "We'll provide you with more escorts for your riders to send word for more soldiers." Oleg and Amrynn nodded.

Aidan turned to Connor and said, "We did get some surprising information after you left. The Aquarians responded to our request for aid . . ."

Connor's eyes narrowed slightly. "And?"

Aidan snickered and replied, "And, they said they would be willing to send soldiers to help! This is the first time since I've been alive that they've actually agreed to help us."

Connor's eyes went wide. "No kidding! Well, maybe there's hope for them after all! What made them decide to be so cordial all of the sudden? They've never agreed to help us before."

Aidan shrugged. "Don't get your hopes up yet. They didn't say *when* they would send soldiers, just that they are agreeable to come to our aid should we need them. I'd say now is that time, so we'll see how they respond."

Connor snorted. "Honestly, it wouldn't surprise me to see them join the Serpens in attacking us."

Aidan nodded. "You're probably not too far off, but I'm not going to turn down any offer for aid now." Aidan leaned back in his chair. "Anyway, as much as it pains me to say it, I must admit that I am needed here more than out on the battlefield. So please, no need to lecture me this time."

Connor smiled and gave him a nod.

The meeting adjourned, and the council members started leaving the chamber. Connor pulled Aidan aside and said, "There's something else . . ."

Aidan looked at Connor with apprehension. He could tell by the tone in his voice that it was not good news.

Connor continued, "Captain Finnian is among those reported missing."

Aidan felt a sinking feeling in the pit of his stomach. He closed his eyes, took a deep breath, and held his composure. He loved Finnian. He loved him like a son, and he fully expected that one day Finnian would marry Reagan and be his son-in-law. He opened his eyes, which were admittedly a little moist, more than they had been prior to closing them. He looked at Connor and said, "He's missing . . . meaning they haven't found his body?"

Connor shook his head. "No, but there a lot of soldiers unaccounted for that are presumed dead. They were still searching the forest for more bodies as I left."

Aidan felt his grief welling up inside of him. He could feel more tears coming into his eyes, so he nodded and said, "Thank you, Connor," and he left the chamber.

The sun was beginning to set below the horizon as Aidan walked out. There was much work to be done, but he was exhausted and now grief-stricken. He needed sleep, but he knew there was no way that was going to happen now. His stomach was in knots, and he felt like he was going to be sick. He took a deep breath and began walking toward the palace. Aidan knew the first thing Reagan would ask as soon as he returned to the palace was if there was any news regarding Finnian. She had been very anxious since Finnian left and was hardly eating.

As he walked up the steps to the palace entrance, he stopped and turned to watch the sunset. The sky was a myriad shades of orange and pink. The beautiful picture in front of him gave him some solace as he tried to compose himself.

After some time, he quietly said to himself, "Finnian, if you're still alive, keep fighting. Come home to us."

A tear rolled down Aidan's cheek. He wiped it with his sleeve and walked through the palace entrance.

As soon as he was inside, he noticed that Reagan had been waiting in the foyer for her father to come home. She began to excitedly walk over to him, but then stopped when she saw his face. She could tell that he had been crying. Terrified, she slowly walked up to him. She said nothing and only stood there staring at him.

Aidan embraced his daughter. He couldn't stand to look at her face as he broke the news to her.

He solemnly said, "There was an attack. Finnian is missing."

Reagan began sobbing into her father's shoulder. Aidan quickly added, "No, no, don't worry. I'm . . ." Aidan had to force the words out. "I'm sure he's fine. Finnian is one of the finest swordsmen in Hume. He can take care of himself." Aidan knew that she could see right through his empty words, but he had to stay strong for his family.

Reagan gave no reply. She only continued to cry into Aidan's shoulder.

Evelyn came into the foyer, and at first, she wasn't sure how to interpret the scene before her. Reagan's arms were wrapped around Aidan's neck with her face buried into one shoulder while she silently sobbed. Evelyn started walking toward the two of them when the realization finally hit her. Something's happened to Finnian.

Evelyn came up behind Reagan and held her along with Aidan. Aidan looked at Evelyn, and the two exchanged a grief-stricken look. Neither spoke, but they each had tears running down their cheeks.

~

Aidan awoke the following morning and watched the sunrise as he stared out his bedroom window. Neither he nor Evelyn had hardly slept at all. Both had cried for most of the night as they mourned for Finnian. Aidan was exhausted, but he pulled himself out of bed anyway. There was too much to do, and Hume needed its king now more than ever.

He tried to force thoughts of Finnian out of his mind and focus on the tasks at hand, but he couldn't. At any moment, Aidan expected to hear the news that Finnian's body had been found.

He decided to go on a morning ride to get some fresh air and try to clear his head, so he quickly got dressed and went outside to the palace stables.

As he was walking toward the stables, he saw a group emerge around the corner, walking toward him. The Aquarian ambassador had just arrived and was being escorted by four palace guards.

The group walked up to Aidan, and the Aquarian gave a slight bow and said, "Good morning, King Aidan. I bring news from Dalip, king of Aquaria."

Aidan nodded and said, "Yes?"

The Aquarian continued, "My king sends his deepest condolences for your circumstances, and he is mustering together some of our finest soldiers to send to Hume."

Aidan sighed and replied, "Well, I certainly appreciate his willingness to help, but do you by any chance know *when* this will be?"

The Aquarian blinked. "No, I do not."

Aidan nodded, biting his lower lip. "Of course you don't. Is it normal for Aquarians to send two different messengers to deliver the same message? Twice now has Dalip sent . . ."

"*King* Dalip," the Aquarian interrupted.

Aidan glared at the Aquarian for a second, then continued, "Twice now has *King* Dalip sent a message to me that he plans on sending soldiers, and not only are they still absent, but he can't even manage to tell me when they will arrive? Meanwhile, Elvenna and Dwarvonia's reinforcements have been here for some time, and they have even already fought against the Serpens." Aidan took a step toward the Aquarian ambassador. "Even the most incompetent army in Andruvia wouldn't take this long to muster active troops. Now tell me, what is *really* going on here?"

The Aquarian's upper lip stiffened and said, "I apologize that you are so . . . dissatisfied with my king, but I *assure* you, there is nothing 'going on,' as you so audaciously assume."

Aidan shook his head. "Then return to your king and don't come back until you have something new to report. I don't have time for this." He turned and mounted his horse as the Aquarian stood and scowled at him.

CAMERON COWBURN

9

THE VAST MAJORITY of Serpenta is one large, arid desert. During the day, it reaches high temperatures that make it almost unbearable for creatures not adapted to its climate. Nighttime is no less hostile, for the temperature has been known to drop as low as freezing temperatures due to the air being so dry, making the sun's heat dissipate quickly after sunset.

However, not all regions of Serpenta are hostile wastelands. In the northwestern region of the province lies its capital city, Tabora. Tabora is located on an oasis with a large lake called Lake Kaivu. The royal palace was built right next to the lake, and it serves as the primary water source for the whole city. The Serpens' bodies require very little water for survival, and the lake has provided them with ample water for ages.

Every building in the city of Tabora is constructed from the same material—a tan-colored type of concrete made from sand, something which the Serpens have in excess. Serpen architecture is very simple, with most of the buildings being a basic cube shape. They typically will have a single door and only one small window per wall. Their buildings are designed solely to be rugged to offer protection from the harsh Serpentan sandstorms that occur mainly during the spring season. The only exception is the Serpen king's palace, a very impressive, extravagant structure with many domes and pillars which sits on the edge of Lake Kaivu.

The Serpens developed their own native language that mainly consists of hissing and snarling, and they are the only people in all of Andruvia that are physically capable of speaking it. They are also able to speak common Andruvian, but with much difficulty, due to the shape of their facial anatomy. They speak common Andruvian with a very heavy accent, and it is actually painful for them to speak it at length because they have to contort their mouths into unnatural positions.

The officer who commanded the Serpen forces during the forest battle is their high commander, Adisa. As soon as Adisa heard the Dwarven horn, he ordered his officers to begin retreating their forces deeper into the forest. They had lost a lot of their warriors in the battle, but rather than being upset, they were genuinely impressed. Adisa was quite pleased to watch the opposing forces adapt to the occasion and show a measure of effectiveness against the Serpens' tactics. They were worthy opponents and had gained a level of Adisa's respect.

Though they suffered heavier losses than expected, they had accomplished the mission their king had given them. It was time to withdraw into Serpenta with their prize.

Adisa had been issuing orders to his officers when he saw one of them pin a Human soldier, who had been rushing one of their wounded, to the ground. Adisa noticed the insignia markings on the Human's armor, and in the Serpen language, yelled, "Stop!" He slithered over and continued, "Look at his insignia. He's an officer. Bind him and we'll bring him as well."

"Yes, High Commander," replied his officer.

They bound Finnian's hands and feet, threw him into a sack, and carried him off as the Serpens disappeared into the forest to make their way back to their homeland.

~

Finnian was extremely disoriented after being bound, gagged, and thrown into a sack. He could hardly comprehend what was happening.

Are they taking me prisoner? he thought. He would have never expected Serpens to take prisoners. From what the Humans knew about them, they seemed like bloodthirsty predators that would kill you as soon as look at you.

He could tell one of them was carrying him over its shoulder like he was a bag of potatoes. Initially, Finnian was furious.

This is humiliating! he thought. *If they're going to kill me, just get it over with!*

He began to thrash and grunt through the gag in his mouth, but his captor quickly swung its fist around and punched him in the small of his back. The punch took his breath away as a wave of pain spread down his spine.

Fair enough . . . he thought.

Resistance would be futile at this point. He was in their custody now, his limbs were bound, and he was unarmed. Judging by the numerous hissing and snarling sounds he could hear, he was surrounded by Serpens. Even if he could escape the sack, what chance would he have of getting away?

After about an hour had passed; he was able to calm his nerves and start thinking rationally. He was struck by how smooth the ride was because the Serpens didn't bounce when they ambulated like two-legged races.

He suddenly felt his carrier drop him onto a hard surface, then he heard other objects being dropped onto the surface around him. These other objects were writhing around, making muffled screams, and he eventually concluded these were other bound prisoners like him.

He heard the rusted *creak* of a gate closing, then he felt like he was moving again, but the ride wasn't as smooth as it had been before.

Finnian nodded and thought, *This is some kind of prisoner transport vehicle. They've captured a bunch of us and are transporting us . . . somewhere.*

This went on for a long time. He could feel the other prisoners around him writhe and roll, and every now and then, there was a muted groan or yell.

Eventually, the air started getting cooler.

It's getting to be dusk. Where are they taking us? To the desert? he wondered.

He could tell by the sound the wheels made that the ground was slowly getting softer. *Sand*, he concluded. *Yes, they're taking us into the Serpentan Desert.*

Further and further they traveled. Finnian was trying to take in as many details about his surroundings as he could. Every little sound, every insignificant detail must be remembered. But as hard as he tried, his mind eventually started to wander.

The first thing that came to his mind was Reagan. He was suddenly felt as though there was a rock in his stomach. He could picture her reaction when she got the news of him being missing.

Finnian knew that he would officially be declared as missing since they would not find his body. He couldn't bear the thought of Reagan being in pain, especially over him.

He took a deep breath and told himself, *Keep it together. You won't get out of this alive if you don't stay focused.* Finnian forced himself to not think about Reagan and continued to analyze the sounds around him.

Finnian started to lose hope of hearing anything useful. The only sound he had heard for some time was the same sound of wheels in sand and occasional hisses and snarls. There were no other sounds to indicate what his location was.

He decided to start recalling the events of the battle. So little is known about the Serpens that this single engagement provided the Humans, Elves, and Dwarves with more information about them than they had collected over the past three ages. The Serpens were obviously intelligent, for they had displayed respectable strategy and tactics during the battle. They weren't primitive reptiles, which was the prevailing opinion.

Finnian stopped for a moment and considered the fact that the Humans had the same opinion about the Orcs, which clearly was incorrect. He shook his head at the haughty attitude they tended to have toward their enemies.

It was questioned whether or not the Serpens could speak the common Andruvian language, but it appeared to Finnian that perhaps they could. The first Serpen he faced off with seemed to understand him when he shouted at it, but of course it may have been a coincidence.

Again, Finnian was struck by a realization. *"It." Why do we refer to a Serpen as "it?"* He shook his head once more.

As his mind played through the events of the battle, the vivid image of Galen's lifeless body lying on the ground flashed into view. Finnian had buried his emotions in the midst of the action as any soldier needs to do, but now they were surfacing. Few people had earned his trust more than Galen, and he was his closest friend.

Being a soldier is a funny thing. You are aware of the ever-present reality of your and your comrades' sudden demise, but you are still unprepared for it when the time comes. As foolish as it was, Finnian never really considered Galen's death to be a possibility. And now that he was gone, Finnian felt blindsided.

He began recalling memories from the past couple of years. He thought of conversations he and Galen shared, their friendly yet competitive sparring matches, and the times they'd fought side by side. He felt a ball in his throat as he struggled to fight back his tears. He took a deep breath, exhaled his anguish, and whispered, "Good-bye, brother."

Finnian resolved to continue to analyze the remainder of the battle for the rest of the journey, which lasted most of the night. They finally came to a stop, and he heard lots of hisses and snarls for several minutes, then heard that distinct *creak* of the gate opening again. Strong arms reached in, picked him up, and carried him out. Finnian heard more muffled yells as the rest of the captives were carried off, and Finnian noticed that they were all being taken in different directions.

They aren't taking us to the same place, he thought.

After being carried for several minutes, Finnian heard the sound of a large, heavy door open and another screech of a metal gate. He saw the top of the sack open, and he was dumped onto a hard concrete floor. Finnian looked all around him and realized he was in a small jail cell. Two Serpens were in the room with him, one holding the sack he was just dumped out of, the other holding a spear to his face.

He was reminded of just how huge they were. His face grew slightly pale when he finally had to admit to himself that defeating that Serpen in the forest in a one-on-one fight was sheer luck.

The Serpen holding the sack suddenly spoke in a language Finnian could comprehend. "I'm going to remove your armor and the bonds from your hands. If you want to keep this spear out of your skull, then I suggest you do not fight." The Serpen's voice was a gruff hiss veiled in a thick and odd accent. He appeared to struggle forming the words with his reptilian mouth.

Finnian's suspicions were confirmed. Not only could they understand common Andruvian, they could speak it fluently.

The Serpen bent down toward Finnian, holding a dagger, and cut the bonds on his hands and slid all his armor off. The bonds on his feet were left in place so he wouldn't be able to run if he tried to fight or escape.

The Serpen left the cell, shut its door, and locked it. Then they both slithered out of the small room and shut the door that was the only way in or out of the room.

Finnian looked around the room. The floor, walls, and ceiling were made of a tan cement-like material. There was a small barred window beyond the cell gate. Finnian considered it for a moment, but then continued with his survey. The window was too small for him to fit through, even without the metal bars, and he had no way of even accessing it. At the front of the small room was a large wooden door with a small window in the center. It was morning now, and the sun was shining through the window, giving the entire room a golden hue. The heat of the day couldn't penetrate the walls, and Finnian was surprised at how pleasantly cool the room was. The cement the Serpens used to build with was an excellent insulator that was designed to protect them from the frigid cold of the night in the Serpentan Desert.

Finnian sat on his cell floor, pondering his situation. *What do they want with us? Why are they keeping us separate?*

Finnian's mind continued to swim through all the possibilities. If he managed to escape, he had no chance of being able to fight his way out. Even if he did, he couldn't survive crossing the Serpentan Desert.

His mind started to consider darker possibilities. *These Serpens are ruthless. They're probably planning on simply torturing and killing every one of us*, he thought.

Then Finnian had another thought that made him shudder. *They're probably carnivores. Are they going to* eat *us? Are we the spoils they brought back for some kind of postbattle feast?*

Finnian fell back onto the cement floor and looked up at the ceiling. He had to face reality. He said aloud to the empty room, "I'm not making it out of here. I'm going to die."

His mind went to Reagan again. He could still see her sitting in the palace library, beautiful auburn hair flowing down over her shoulders. Tears began to fill his eyes as he covered his face with his hands.

"What have I done?" he said. "Why was I so stubborn!"

Finnian began to recollect all the memories from his past two years with Reagan. They had been the happiest two years of his life. He had procrastinated in marrying her because he thought he would always have time for that after his career as a soldier was over. He had been so fixated on fighting and not being "distracted" from his duties that he had ignored something else—the adopted family he'd had for the past four years. He had always longed for the family he lost when he was a boy, and he foolishly neglected the loving family he had now. Reagan, Aidan, Evelyn, and Owen were his family. He loved Aidan and Evelyn as much as he had loved his own parents. He loved Owen like a younger brother. And Reagan . . . Reagan was the woman he knew he wanted to spend the rest of his days loving, cherishing, and supporting. But now . . . now he would never get the chance. He had told himself that he was only fighting to protect Hume, his homeland. But deep down, he knew that was a lie. He was fighting for vengeance over the death of his father and mother. He had been holding onto his bitterness and resentment, refusing to let it go since he was a child. He spent so much time trying to avenge what he had lost that he ignored what he had gained.

For the first time since his mother died when he was fourteen, Finnian began to cry. He hadn't slept since the night prior to the forest battle, and he eventually fell asleep on the cell floor.

~

Finnian was awoken by the sound of the wooden door opening. He sprang awake and saw two Serpens entering the room. One was carrying two small items in his hands, the other was carrying a spear.

He couldn't tell if these were the same Serpens he met earlier, for they all looked similar to him.

The Serpen carrying the small items said in the same gruff voice as before, "Sit there peacefully and you will keep your life."

Finnian nodded. The Serpens opened the cell door and laid the two items on the floor inside the cell. Finnian realized the items were bread and meat wrapped in cloth and a container full of drinking water. The Serpens closed the cell door and left the room without saying anything else.

The bread appeared to be quite stale. The meat was raw and consisted of short, thin strips, as though it came from some small indigenous animal.

Finnian didn't care. He was hungry and dehydrated, and he was very thankful for the food and water. He crawled toward the items on the cell floor and devoured the food and gulped the water down without a second thought. Nothing had ever tasted so good to him.

After finishing his meal, Finnian considered the implications of his captors bringing him food and water.

They obviously want me alive, but for what purpose? he thought. He started putting all the pieces together. *They captured multiple prisoners, brought us back to Serpenta, they're keeping us isolated without any contact with one another, and they want us alive. They plan to interrogate us.*

Finnian felt a slight chill down his spine, for he knew that with interrogation often came torture . . .

Not long after the food and water were brought in, the same duo of Serpens return once more. The same Serpen spoke again. "Stand in the far corner and face the wall. I'm going to tie your hands and you will be put back into the sack. If you move, you die."

Finnian complied with the Serpen's instructions. After all, what choice did he have?

They carried him out of the room and Finnian thought, *At least I'm about to find out what they intend to do with me. No more guessing.* Now that the moment of truth was upon him, he couldn't help but let his mind drift to Reagan once more. He pictured her face from the last time he saw her.

He whispered under his breath, "I'm sorry, Reagan."

Finnian could tell the exact moment he was carried outside. He was slammed with a wall of intense heat like he had never felt before. He immediately started feeling beads of sweat form on his forehead.

Soon after being brought outside, he was carried back into a different building. He could feel the immediate drop in temperature and was thankful for it. He was dropped on another hard floor and was taken out of the sack.

He was in a much larger room, and there were six Serpens present. Four of them stood in each corner holding a spear and were presumably guards. The other two stood at the center of the room next to a small wooden chair.

It's definitely an interrogation, he thought. The Serpens would have no other use for a chair designed for a Human body.

He was carried over by one of the guards and sat in the chair facing the two Serpens in the center of the room. Finnian noticed that one of them had the same silver band around his neck like the one he saw in the forest and assumed this must signify rank. In fact, this Serpen *was* the same one he met in the forest. He was Adisa, the high commander of the Serpen Army.

The other Serpen was wearing something different entirely. He wore a beautiful elaborate necklace made of gold and precious stones, something only fit for royalty. The rest of his body, like every other Serpen he had seen, was unclothed. Besides his apparel, there were no other features to distinguish him from the rest.

He stared at Finnian for quite some time. Finnian started to get chills as he looked back into those reptilian eyes. There was something quite eerie about them, something Finnian would have struggled to describe. The eyes were clearly distinct from a Human's with their slit pupils, but conveyed within them was a sense of dignity. There was intelligence. There was honor. This Serpen that stood before Finnian had a presence about him that demanded respect.

The Serpen finally spoke in a similar gruff hissing voice. "Good morning, officer. I am Zesiro, king of Serpenta."

Finnian was speechless. He was face-to-face with the king of the Serpens. Furthermore, he knew that Finnian was an officer.

Finnian eventually responded, "How did you know that I am an officer?"

"The markings on the armor you wore indicate you hold a high rank, do they not?" replied Zesiro.

Finnian was quite surprised. The Serpens obviously know a lot more about the Humans than he had expected.

"Yes, they do," Finnian finally said.

Zesiro continued, "What is your name?"

Finnian considered this for a moment, then eventually concluded there wasn't any harm in giving his real name at this point. "I am Captain Finnian of the Human Army," he replied.

Zesiro nodded and began to approach Finnian as he spoke. "I'm looking for answers, Captain Finnian . . . answers I will have one way or another. I decided I would begin with you because you are the highest-ranking officer we've captured, and therefore I assume you possess the most knowledge."

Zesiro stopped directly in front of Finnian and glared at him. "The methods I use to obtain these answers is entirely up to you. This can be very simple, or . . ." Zesiro inched in close to Finnian's face. "Very unpleasant for you."

There it was. Finnian had the confirmation he was waiting for. That's why he and the others were brought here—interrogation and torture. Finnian drew a deep breath. He was prepared for whatever evils they had prepared for him. He would never give these snakes any information. He simply stared directly into Zesiro's sinister yellow eyes and said nothing.

Zesiro backed up and stood up straight, still looking at Finnian. He eventually broke off his glare, slithered over to the left side of the room, and stared out the small window.

Still looking out the window, he said, "My soul is burdened, Captain. I simply do not understand, so help me, will you?"

Finnian was perplexed. Interrogation was something he was somewhat familiar with. It was practiced by both the Union and the

CAMERON COWBURN

Orcovans. The Serpen king's approach to interrogation started as it typically did—threaten and intimidate the subject. But now, the mood was changing. Instead of a continued display of bravado designed to intimidate, Zesiro was allowing himself to become vulnerable.

Zesiro continued, "Besides our guards protecting our border when you violate it"—he glanced at Finnian, then back out the window—"Hume and Serpenta have cohabited in Andruvia peacefully for many generations." Zesiro turned and faced Finnian. "Why, then, would you want to violate that peace? What do you have to gain?"

Finnian was at a loss for words. He hadn't the slightest idea of what Zesiro was referring to. He answered in a forceful tone, "The Humans violated nothing."

"No?" replied Zesiro. He turned to Adisa and made several hissing sounds.

Adisa quickly slithered over to Finnian and coiled around his body, constricting it tightly. He felt as though someone was standing on his chest as the air was forced out of his lungs. It was a feeling unlike anything he had ever felt before.

Zesiro slithered over to Finnian and said with much more volume and force, "The Humans violated nothing? You know exactly what you did, and I need to know why! What could you possibly have to gain!"

Adisa loosened some, allowing Finnian to finally breathe and answer the question.

Finnian drew in a deep breath and began panting, his body trying to recover from its oxygen deprivation. Still gasping for air, he said, "I . . . have no . . . idea . . . what you're . . . talking about."

Zesiro inched in close to Finnian's face again. "You know *exactly* what I'm talking about." He turned to one of the guards in the corner and let out a series of hisses and snarls. The guard exited through the door to the outside.

Zesiro turned back to Finnian. "Human assassins infiltrated my palace courtyard using the lake and murdered my son, Prince Dakiri!"

Finnian couldn't believe his ears! He had never heard such an incredulous accusation! He was about to respond when the door opened and the guard returned carrying a body. He threw the body on the floor at Finnian's feet.

The smell was rancid. The body had obviously been dead for some time. Finnian looked at it and immediately recognized it was wearing Human patrol armor.

Zesiro yelled as loud as his reptilian larynx was able, "There are twenty-nine others like this one that riddled my seven-year-old son with arrows as he was playing in the courtyard! This is Human armor, is it not!? Do *not* tell me the Humans have violated nothing!"

Finnian couldn't believe what he was seeing. It was indeed Human armor, and this body had been dead much longer than anyone that had been killed in yesterday's battle. Another oddity was that it was wearing patrol armor, not battle armor.

Finnian studied the decaying body. Something seemed off about it . . . Then suddenly, he put all of the pieces together.

"The missing patrols!" he exclaimed out loud. "This is the armor from the missing patrols!" Furthermore, the body in the armor wasn't Human, it was Aquarian!

Finnian excitedly looked at Zesiro. "I can explain what happened! The Humans didn't do this!" Zesiro watched him skeptically as he continued, "This is not a Human body! Look at its complexion. Look at the hands—they're too broad for Human hands. Compare them to mine!"

All the Serpens in the room looked at one another with confused looks. Zesiro finally hissed an order at Adisa, who was still wrapped around Finnian, and he uncoiled. They all inspected Finnian's hands and then the body's hands.

Finnian continued, "We had three of our patrols go missing without a single trace over the past month, and we have been at a loss for an explanation. The Aquarians must have ambushed our patrols, took their armor, and assassinated your son. They framed us!"

There was still visible confusion on the faces of the Zesiro and Adisa. They began to speak in their Serpentan language, "My king, this does explain some of the questions we've had. For instance, it explains why the assassins' armor showed signs of previous damage before we killed them. And after comparing, there *is* a discernible difference between the hands on the body and the captain's hands. It never occurred to me that the bodies may not even be Human. They all look so much alike that I can't tell them apart."

The Serpens have had minimal contact with the other races in Andruvia. They are a proud, self-sufficient people that have had little interest in foreign relations. Because of their minimal exposure to the other races, they had a difficult time discerning their physical differences. Even more so, they simply had no interest in taking the time to learn those differences.

There was a pause as Zesiro considered Adisa's comments, then responded in Serpentan, "Go and inspect the rest of the bodies for the same type of hands and compare them to the rest of our Human prisoners. Return when you have finished." Adisa nodded and began to slither toward the door.

Zesiro turned and addressed Finnian as Adisa left the room. "Captain, explain this again."

Finnian took a deep breath. "All right. I'm a Human patrol captain. Over the past month, we had three of our ten-man patrols vanish without a trace. We assumed they were captured or killed by our enemies, the Orcovans . . ."

Zesiro held up his hand, motioning for Finnian to stop. "The Humans are at war with the Orcovans?"

Finnian replied, "Well, yes. The entire Andruvian Union, Humans, Elves, and Dwarves, have been at war with them for a long time."

Zesiro nodded thoughtfully, then said, "Continue."

Finnian picked up where he left off, "The armor this body is wearing is Human patrol armor. It is not the armor we would wear into battle. Compare it to the armor you confiscated from me. Compare it to every Human soldier your warriors fought yesterday. Patrol armor is lightweight and designed for riding on a horse all day, not for protection in a battle. Even if we *did* try to assassinate your son, we wouldn't wear that armor. And this body isn't even Human. It's an Aquarian. They must have attacked our patrols, killed our men, and took their armor to frame us for assassinating your son."

Zesiro focused on Finnian for a long time. He finally shook his head and said, "Why would the Aquarians go to this kind of trouble to frame Hume for murdering my son?"

Finnian responded, "There's always been tension between our provinces. Aquaria was once part of Hume during the First Age, but we had . . . disagreements. They didn't agree with the government's policies, we have some of the best farmlands in all of Andruvia, and we have many freshwater lakes. They have coveted our land for ages. There was a civil war that ended heavily in our favor. We granted them their independence as a sovereign state, but they have been required to pay taxes to Hume. There has been a lot of tension between our provinces ever since."

Finnian paused, and then added, "We never considered them to be a threat because their army is the weakest of all the Andruvian provinces."

Just then, Adisa returned from inspecting the rest of the bodies. He approached Zesiro and in Serpentan said, "All of the bodies have the broader hands, just like the captain said. I never knew there was a physical difference between the Humans and the Aquarians other than their propensity for water. My king, it *does* appear that all the bodies from the assassins we killed are a different race from the Humans we captured."

Zesiro nodded and responded in Serpentan, "This would also explain how they were able to cross Lake Kaivu so easily. If what the captain told me is true, there's bad blood between the Aquarians and the Humans."

Adisa looked at Finnian, then back at Zesiro. "What are your orders, my king?"

Zesiro slithered over to the window and stared out, deep in thought. Finally, he returned to Adisa and said, "Take the captain back to his cell and feed him and the others again. Tomorrow morning I'll have an answer for you."

Adisa bowed and said, "Yes, my king."

Finnian sat and watched in suspense as the two Serpens had their conversation in their native tongue. It was very frustrating to see them decide his fate in an open conversation when he couldn't understand a single syllable.

Adisa gave the order to the guards, and they put Finnian back in the sack and returned him to his cell.

Finnian sat in his cell and replayed the day's events over and over in his head.

It all makes sense now, he thought. *The Serpens invaded Hume because they thought we assassinated the prince. Then, they took some of us hostage to be interrogated about our motives for the assassination.*

Finnian spit on the floor and thought, *Aquarians. Conniving dogs.* He shook his head. *I can't believe they would do this. Hundreds of people dead, and for what! Vengeance?*

Just then, Finnian felt a twinge of conviction. He was a hypocrite.

Not unlike the vengeance you've spent your whole life wanting for the Orcs killing your parents . . . he thought.

Finnian felt thoroughly humbled. Vengeance is a fool's game. Instead of atoning for wrongdoing, it simply brings more pain and suffering.

Finnian lay down on the cell floor and stared at the blue sky through the small window in the wall. He was still sleep-deprived, and it had been an exhausting day. He eventually fell asleep.

10

COMMANDER CONNOR HAD arranged for an entire regiment containing five full battalions to be deployed south to reinforce the survivors from the forest battle. Their orders were to secure and protect the border, and almost all of them were very anxious to leave. None of them relished the thought of resting comfortably at Enlanor while others were out fighting and dying.

The Elves and the Dwarves each arranged to send two more of their own battalions to Hume to aid the securing of the southern border.

The evacuation of civilians in the southern region of Hume was started immediately. In fact, many took it upon themselves to evacuate as soon as the word of Serpen attacks reached their villages. They were all being temporarily relocated to the safety of the capital, Enlanor.

As Commander Connor and the regiment were preparing to depart, King Aidan rode up beside him in full battle dress. Connor gave him a small smile and shook his head.

"You're too predictable, my king," he said.

Aidan furrowed his brow and replied, "I would begin to question your tactical reasoning if you didn't expect me to join my men! Besides, there was no way I was going to let *you* get all the glory!"

Connor smiled, then added, "I'm truly sorry about Captain Finnian. We'll make sure they pay for this."

Aidan shook his head and said, "There's been too much death as it is. We don't need any more."

Aidan and Connor exchanged a nod. Connor gave the word to sound the horn for their departure.

Almost every soul in Enlanor was watching as their loved ones rode off in the great throng of soldiers and horses. They played music, they blew kisses, and they cheered as the soldiers left to defend their homeland. However, behind all the celebration was the awful feeling that it may be the last time they ever saw them.

~

At the time the regiment was leaving Enlanor, a Human platoon was in the middle of its patrol along the northeast border with Orcova. The sky was cloudy, and Lieutenant Declan's platoon was thankful for the shade from the scorching sun.

Lieutenant Declan was a young, but capable, officer in the Northern Hume patrol. He was raised in a family of men who all spent the entirety of their careers in the Human Army, and he had been expected to do the same since childhood.

He had been in the Northern Hume patrol for almost a year now, and he had originally requested to be assigned to the northern patrol, hoping he would be able to fight alongside the accomplished swordsman Finnian. Finnian's fighting skills and competency as a leader were well-known among those in the Hume patrol, and Declan hoped to learn much from him. He was disappointed when he was placed in Captain Edmond's company instead of Finnian's, but he was grateful for his opportunity to lead a platoon with so little experience, and Captain Edmond was a superb leader in his own right.

It had been an uneventful patrol thus far. In fact, the northern patrols had seen no signs of any Orcovan activity for some time. Some were on edge over this, suspecting that the Orcovans were on the verge of doing something big, but Declan tried to be optimistic. He fantasized that perhaps the Orcovans were growing weary of fighting and have taken a hiatus from their constant efforts to attack the northern patrols, but he knew that was just wishful thinking. The Orcovans have never been known to be a people who grew weary of fighting. They lived for the "glory" of combat, and they were very good at it.

There was a lot of unrest among the men in the platoon this morning. Most of them could only think about how they were stuck patrolling while an entire regiment was marching south to beat back the Serpens.

The news of the Serpen attack was of course met with shock, but most of the soldiers also saw it as an opportunity for a new challenge. They wanted the reputation of being a soldier who fought the "mighty snake people," and Lieutenant Declan was struggling to keep morale up.

The platoon came to the top of a large hill that overlooked a valley to the northeast Orcovan border. Declan thought this would be a good spot to stop and give the horses a short rest and water break.

As they came over the crest of the hill, the entire platoon stopped dead in their tracks. There was an enormous mass of Orcs filling the valley, and they were marching straight toward them.

The lieutenant gasped and removed his helmet, staring out over the valley. In an odd way, it was almost beautiful—the order, the precision.

One of his sergeants stammered, "There must be at least ten thousand strong!"

Declan looked at the sergeant and said, "At *least* . . ." He looked back out over the valley. He was half in awe, half in shock. "This is it. This is the invasion we were expecting. It's finally here . . ."

Suddenly, the platoon saw hundreds of small projectiles launch into the air from the mass of Orcs nearest to them.

The sergeant grabbed Declan by the shoulder and yelled, "Lieutenant, we are in bow range! We need to get out of here, now!"

Declan turned around and shouted, "*Move! Move! Move!*" but before the soldiers could respond, they were slammed by a hail of arrows. Their light patrol armor was no match for the power of Orcovan bows.

Declan felt as though he got hit with a hammer in his abdomen and chest, and he fell off his horse and onto the ground. A searing, burning pain filled his chest and abdomen, and he struggled for breath. He looked down at his torso and saw two thick arrow shafts protruding out from his pierced armor.

Every man and horse in the platoon toppled to the ground, riddled with arrows. There were scattered screams and moans of pain as those who were still alive tried to stand up and run, but none were able.

It wasn't long before the Orcs leading the pack reached the location of the dying platoon. They wasted no time finishing off the survivors.

Declan lay on the ground, gasping for breath and bleeding from his arrow wounds. Every breath was met with a wet cough that spewed a fine mist of blood.

An Orc casually walked up and stood over him. Declan looked up at him and could see merciless eyes staring out from behind the helmet back at him.

The Orc raised his spear and thrust it into Declan's chest, and his body went limp. The warrior withdrew his spear from Declan's body and continued marching southwest toward Enlanor.

11

ZESIRO AROSE IN the morning and decided to go to the palace courtyard on the shore of Lake Kaivu. Captain Finnian's story was outlandish, but it did offer explanations to his questions: Why were the assassins' armor already damaged? How did the assassins accomplish the crossing of the lake to get to the courtyard? Why would Hume attempt to assassinate Prince Dakiri unprovoked? How did the Humans infiltrate Serpenta without being noticed when, unbeknownst to the Humans, they regularly monitor the border between the two provinces? All were questions Zesiro had wrestled with.

He shook his head at his foolishness for not thinking the Aquarian border needed to be monitored as closely. The Serpens had concluded long ago that the Aquarians were a feeble kingdom that posed no threat to Serpenta, plus Tabora was so close to the border that there was already a very strong military presence nearby to intervene should it be necessary.

He couldn't deny that every one of the assassins did appear to be a different race from the Humans they had captured from the first battle. He personally inspected each body after the interrogation with Finnian, and though the differences between the races are subtle, they could be plainly seen when you knew what to look for. Zesiro stared out over the calm waters of the lake as he thought about his son, Dakiri.

Dakiri was the royal heir of King Zesiro and Queen Arjana. Serpen young hatch from eggs, and there can be as many as thirty eggs in a single litter. The first male to hatch is the heir to the family line and would be raised within the home. Because Dakiri was the heir of the royal family line, he would have been the next king of Serpenta. The remaining males would not have any right to be heirs and would instead be raised to be warriors. They would have no connection with their parents whatsoever and would live their lives without knowing who their parents even were. Their only family was their brothers-in-arms, and these warriors share a camaraderie that was unrivaled across all Andruvia.

The females of the litter would also be raised without knowing their biological parents, but they would be laborers instead of warriors. Serpentan females were responsible for harvesting food and water, building, and crafting. They were the backbone of Serpen civilization, and they were treated with the utmost respect. The warrior males, on the other hand, were thought of as expendable drones in Serpen society.

While seemingly harsh, the societal opinion of the warriors was actually intentional. Serpen leadership decided long ago to instill that sense of alienation in the warriors. They were born and bred for one purpose, and they had little to lose. Without the distraction of family ties, they would be more efficient and bold fighters.

If the king should die with no living royal heir to take his place, a new royal family would be elected by the Serpentan citizens. Because of this law, assassinations of the royal heirs have occurred intermittently throughout Serpentan history. Therefore, the royal heirs would often be confined to the palace grounds by the parents for their protection until the time to assume the throne came.

Prince Dakiri was a bright, cheerful child of seven years, and Zesiro and Arjana loved him dearly. Dakiri would spend most of his free time in the palace courtyard near Lake Kaivu because it was the only location he was allowed to explore outside. The courtyard was enclosed within strong thirty-foot walls on all sides but one—the side facing the lake. The walls extended one hundred feet into the water. The Serpens were not strong swimmers, and the courtyard's architects never considered swimming across the large lake to be a credible security risk.

Dakiri spent so much time in the courtyard that the assassins had no trouble predicting a general time period when the prince would be vulnerable. They entered the far side of the lake in the late afternoon and swam submerged across the lake, only coming up for breath occasionally. They arrived near the opening in the wall to the courtyard in the late evening when they knew the prince would be outside playing before it was time to retire to the palace for the night. When they saw their opportunity, they swam submerged up to the shore armed with bows, quickly emerged from the water, and released as many arrows at the young prince as they could before the palace guards reacted and killed each of them.

It had been a suicide mission, and it was one that each of them was proud to volunteer for. The Aquarians have coveted the province of Hume for many generations. They are an impoverished culture, and their swampy province of Aquaria was slowly running out of resources. The Aquarians harbor so much bitterness toward the Humans that they would rather die than consider any alliance with them in the Andruvian Union.

The oasis where Tabora, Serpenta's capital, resides is not far from the Aquarian border. The Aquarians discovered the city during their exploration into the desert, and they had been stealthily surveying it for the past two decades. They used Lake Kaivu as their means to get close enough to gather information and not be detected by the Serpens.

After Prince Dakiri was born, they quickly realized that they would easily be able to assassinate him from the lake, and they hatched their nefarious plan to get revenge on Hume.

It was obvious to them during their surveillance of Tabora that the military might of the Serpens exceeded that of the entire Andruvian Union. In sheer numbers alone, they were able to match the number of military personnel in the entire Union. If the Aquarians could start a war between Serpenta and the Union, Serpenta would most assuredly be the victors. Hume would then be crippled, and the climate of Hume is too cold for the Serpens, so they would return to the desert after the war was over. Hume would then be ripe for the plucking by the Aquarians. They suspected the Orcovans would have also been contenders to colonize Hume, but they were naively confident some kind of agreement with the Orcs could be met. After all, the Orcs would be indebted to the Aquarians for toppling the Union.

The only factor they had to be patient with was the weather. They needed to wait for a summer that was hot enough. The Serpens are cold-blooded, and they get sluggish in colder weather. Had the Aquarians sparked the war during a colder year, the Serpens would not be as effective in battle when they left their desert, and they may not have been victorious. The Aquarians waited for the perfect time, and this abnormally warm summer of 1127 of the Fourth Age was it.

Zesiro still remembered that fateful evening vividly. He and Arjana were in the palace when they suddenly heard a commotion coming from the courtyard. They made their way to the palace exit when a guard suddenly burst through the doors and yelled to every other available guard in the palace, "We're being attacked! Everyone to the courtyard, *now*!"

Zesiro and Arjana looked at each other in horror, for they knew that Dakiri had been in the courtyard. Zesiro bolted toward the exit, and it took three guards to hold him back. He screamed and clawed at the door, but the guards were able to restrain him until all the assassins were dead.

Zesiro and Arjana were finally allowed to leave the palace after the guards had ensured the area was clear and secure, and the image both of them saw will forever be ingrained in their memories. They saw Dakiri's lifeless body lying on the shore of the lake with at least twenty arrows protruding from it.

Arjana immediately buried her face into Zesiro's chest and wailed loudly. Zesiro could do nothing but stare in shock at the horrifying scene before him. Never has a father's anger burned more furiously than on that night, and Zesiro was consumed with grief and a thirst for justice. He and Arjana could have another litter of children and establish a new heir to the throne, but Dakiri could never be replaced in their hearts.

One might assume that Serpens wouldn't develop a loving bond with their children because of their unorthodox family customs, but nothing is further from the truth. The identities of the parents of each non-heir Serpen is kept secret for this very reason.

Serpens do not possess the ability to shed tears, but if they did, Zesiro would have shed every ounce of water in his body as he recollected that night.

"I *must* know the truth!" he said aloud. "I owe it to Dakiri!"

Zesiro knew what he must do, and he turned and slithered back into the palace.

~

Finnian awoke that morning in his cell and sat pondering what the day would bring. He wondered if the Serpens would actually believe that Hume was not responsible for the assassination. He wondered if he and the rest of the Human captives would ever make it out of Serpenta alive. And, he wondered if he'd ever see Reagan again.

Shortly after he awoke, his two regular Serpen guards entered his room and brought him the same standard meal they had previously brought.

One of them said, "Eat quickly. King Zesiro wishes to speak to you immediately."

Finnian nodded and consumed his breakfast as fast as his stomach would allow him.

He was, as usual, put in the sack and carried to the same interrogation room where Zesiro and Adisa were already waiting for him. He was set into the chair in the middle of the room, and the two Serpens stared at him for a long time before speaking. Finnian wished he could read Serpentan facial expressions. He couldn't tell if they were about to question him again or skewer him with a spear.

Zesiro finally spoke. "Captain, you have claimed that the Aquarians are framing Hume for the assassination of my son, Prince Dakiri. Tell me again why the Aquarians would want to do this."

Finnian nodded. He would have been annoyed at having to tell the story for a third time, but he knew this was a typical interrogation tactic. Make the victim retell their story multiple times and listen for any differences in details, which may indicate deception.

He began, "There has always been enmity between our provinces. We defeated them in a war during the First Age, and they have never let go of their malice. Our foreign relations with Aquaria have been very tense, and there have been instances where they have even threatened to attack our patrols that have gotten 'too close' to their border, according to them. They want our land, and it looks like they wanted you to do the dirty work for them, so they framed us for murdering your son."

Adisa replied, "We have captured seven other Human soldiers from the battle in the forest, some officers, some lower-ranking soldiers, and I have personally interviewed them regarding this issue. We kept all of you separate from each other without any contact, and you have all given similar accounts, even under . . . *great duress.*"

Adisa and Zesiro exchanged a knowing look. Zesiro then added, "This means one of two things: Either you are all ignorant of the acts committed by your own government, or what you are saying is in fact true."

Zesiro slithered over to the window in the room and stared out. He continued, "We intend to find out which one it is. Therefore, this is what is going to happen: You alone will be transported back to the Human border, and you will be set free. You will contact your superiors and inform them that I wish to meet with them. Two days from now at midday, they are to meet me at the location of the small village we attacked a few days ago. They may bring their entire army with them if it makes them feel more comfortable. If they do not show . . ." Zesiro turned and faced Finnian. "I will unleash a fury on your province like you've never seen before. Is that clear?"

Finnian could barely even breathe. He was going to be released! He opened his mouth and managed to stammer, "Yes, King Zesiro." He paused for a moment, then added, "What about the other Humans you captured?"

Zesiro nodded and said, "We will bring them with us to the meeting. Depending on how the meeting plays out, they *may* be released back to Hume. Anything else?"

Finnian could barely hide his excitement, but he tried to focus and think of any other questions. He finally asked, "When do I leave?"

"Right now," replied Zesiro. He turned to the guards in the room and made several hissing and snarling sounds. They put Finnian back into the sack and was carried outside. He heard the familiar creak of a metal gate opening, and he knew he was being loaded back into the cart in which he was brought to Serpenta.

The heat of the desert was almost unbearable, and it was made worse by being wrapped in a heavy sack. Finnian could feel sweat pouring out of every pore in his body, but his spirits stayed high. He could hardly believe he was being set free, for he had every expectation that he was going to die in Serpenta.

Finnian noticed now more than the ride into Serpenta that the cart was traveling quite fast. He wondered if it was being pulled by some beast of burden or by the Serpens themselves. Finnian knew all too well from the forest battle that they are certainly capable of speeds much greater than that of a Human.

One thing Zesiro said troubled Finnian: "Either you are all ignorant of the acts committed by your own government, or you are telling the truth." Finnian knew Aidan better than anyone else outside of the royal family, and he could never believe Aidan would give the order to assassinate the Serpentan prince. However, was it possible there was a conspiracy between the Aquarians and another high-ranking official in the Union?

Finnian shook his head. Would a cat conspire with a mouse?

He couldn't perceive a scenario where an Aquarian would ever get along well enough with a Human, Elf, or Dwarf to conspire together.

Finnian assumed it wouldn't be difficult to find the Human military when he got to the border. It's standard protocol to secure the border when an attack from foreign invaders occurs.

I just have to get a horse and find Aidan and Connor, he thought.

Finnian thought it best to take Zesiro up on his offer to bring as many soldiers as they could spare to the meeting. There was of course the possibility of the entire meeting being a trap to lure Hume's highest-ranking officials out of Enlanor, but even if it was a trap, fighting the Serpens at Dunsbury was preferable to fighting them in Enlanor.

Finally, Finnian's mind drifted to Reagan. He would actually have the chance to see her again! He needed to see her. He needed to apologize for his foolishness. He wasn't going to delay marrying her one moment more. His heart began to race in anticipation, but then Finnian stopped himself and shook his head, frustrated.

Stay focused! Now is not the time to daydream! he thought. As determined as he was, he still struggled to keep his mind focused for the remainder of the trip to Hume.

~

Finnian felt the cart come to a stop and heard the creaking of the gate to the cart opening. He was lifted out of the cart and dumped out onto the hot yellow sand. The brightness of the sun reflecting off the sand was blinding, and it took his eyes a moment to adjust.

As Finnian's eyes finally adjusted, he saw the cart he had been transported in these last few days was pulled by none other than the Serpens themselves. It had a flatbed enclosed with a cage that was supported by two large, very wide wheels that would easily tread across the desert sand. There was a yoke at the front wide enough for two adult Serpens to push the cart forward.

Finnian took a survey of the landscape, and he noticed they were sitting at the base of a large sand dune with nothing but miles of desert in every other direction.

There were ten Serpens with him—two to push the cart and eight as armed escorts. One of them looked at Finnian, and while motioning to the tall dune, said in the typical raspy Serpen voice, "The border is just on the other side of this sand dune. Your soldiers will spot you shortly after coming over its crest, so you won't have to travel far." The Serpen then handed him a bladder of water, a gesture that surprised him.

Finnian didn't even hesitate. He grabbed the bladder, removed the cap, and drained it within seconds. Finnian volunteered a small "Thank you," as he handed the empty bladder back. All ten of the Serpens nodded in return.

He turned and started to climb. His feet sunk into the sand with every step, and he quickly became envious of the Serpens' bodies that could glide easily across the desert sand.

The heat of the desert was agony. As he finally reached the top of the sand dune, he looked out before him and he saw the Foyle River, which is the dividing line between Hume and Serpenta. Off in the distance beyond the river, he saw the start of the very familiar prairies of Southern Hume with numerous companies of Human soldiers guarding the border. Finnian practically laughed out loud at the beautiful sight of his homeland, and he started racing down the sand dune.

~

Captain Martin of the southern Human patrol was leading one of the companies charged with protecting the southern border. Every southern civilian had been evacuated to Enlanor, and everything had been quiet since the battle. It seemed as though the Serpens had simply attacked the battalions in the forest, then fled back to Serpenta.

After what remained of the battalions from the forest battle were reinforced, the forces dispersed and pushed south until they reached the border, and not a single living Serpen was found. They had vanished without a trace. The soldiers' standing orders were to keep the border secure until further notice.

Some of the men in Captain Martin's company spotted a figure appear over the large sand dune in the distance. An alarm was immediately raised, and everyone in the company began to prepare for battle.

Martin rode to the front line and watched the figure slowly descend the sand dune. He yelled out, "Archers, hold your fire! We only engage if it crosses the border."

The men were watching with anticipation when Martin suddenly said, "That's no Serpen! It's walking on two legs . . . That's a man!" He began to shout, "Stand down! That's a man! Stand down!"

Martin called for the nearest sergeant, and Sergeant Brennan quickly ran over to him.

After he arrived, Martin said, "Brennan, you and three of your men take that man into custody for questioning as soon as he reaches the river. I want to speak to him personally!"

"Yes, sir," replied Brennan, and he turned to three soldiers who were standing next to him, one of whom happened to be Private Kieran. Brennan instructed them to follow him down to the Foyle River to take this desert wanderer into custody, and they quickly rode their horses down to the river and retrieve him.

As the wandering man was nearing the river, two of the four soldiers drew their bows and said, "Hold! Drop any weapons you're carrying and approach slowly!"

The man held up his hands to show he was unarmed and replied, "I am Captain Finnian of the Northern Hume patrol! I have an urgent message for King Aidan and Commander Connor!"

The four soldiers looked at each other in complete shock.

"Captain Finnian?" replied Kieran. "Wha . . . How did you . . ." He had difficulty even putting a sentence together. "What happened! Everyone thought you were dead!"

Finnian jumped into the river and plunged his face into the water and gulped as much of it as his stomach could hold. Despite the offering of water from the Serpen, he was still quite dehydrated. They waded into the river to help Finnian over to the Hume side of the river bank.

After they had reached the far bank, Finnian said, "I need to speak with King Aidan and Commander Connor immediately. I need a horse to get to Enlanor."

Brennan replied, "Actually, Captain, the king and the commander are here. Their command post is set up near Dunsbury."

"Excellent! I need someone to take me to them immediately," replied Finnian.

"Yes, sir," Sergeant Brennan replied.

Finnian did a double-take when he looked at Kieran. "I know you . . . I talked with you just prior to the battle, didn't I?"

Kieran nodded and said, "Yes, sir. Private Kieran."

Finnian nodded with a slight smile. "Right. I'm glad you made it, Kieran."

"Likewise, sir," said Kieran.

The group traveled from the river bank and reported to Captain Martin. Martin nearly fell off his horse when he saw Finnian.

"Finnian! We all thought you were dead! What happened? Why were you wandering in the Serpentan Desert!"

"I was captured during the battle in the forest and they transported me and seven others to Tabora."

"You were taken to Tabora? No Human has ever set foot in that city before!" replied Martin. "How did you escape?"

Finnian replied, "I didn't. They let me go." Finnian cleared his throat. "I'm sorry, Martin, but I really must speak to Aidan and Connor as soon as possible. I can catch you up with everything that happened in Serpenta later."

Martin nodded and said, "Oh, of course! Forgive me. I'll arrange an escort that will take you straight to them. Do you need water or food?"

Finnian paused at the thought of food. He *was* quite hungry, but he resisted the temptation and resolved to deliver Zesiro's message first.

"Just some water. Thank you," he replied.

Martin nodded and handed him his own canteen.

Kieran had heard every word of Finnian's and Martin's exchange. He could hardly believe his ears! Captain Finnian was not only captured by the Serpens and taken to their capital, but they actually released him!

What I wouldn't give to hear the whole story! he thought. He watched in amazement as Finnian was escorted off toward Dunsbury.

Dunsbury wasn't far from the Serpentan border where Finnian crossed. After a few hours of riding, they arrived at the command post situated just outside of what was now the ghost town of Dunsbury.

Aidan stepped outside his tent when he heard the commotion, and he saw a crowd hovering around the riders who just arrived. Aidan began walking up to the crowd when he suddenly felt as though his heart had stopped.

"Could that be . . . No, it can't be . . . *Yes!* It is!" Aidan yelled, *"Finnian!"* and sprinted toward the weathered-looking man sitting on one of the horses.

Finnian heard someone shout his name and turned his head toward the noise. He saw Aidan running toward him, and he quickly dismounted and ran out to meet his king.

Aidan embraced Finnian and said, "I thought we lost you, boy!" Aidan held the hug for almost a minute while he shed tears of joy. He had been mourning the loss of a son for the past few days, and now that son was back from the grave! He finally looked at Finnian and said, "What happened! Where were you?"

Finnian said, "Get Connor and let's meet somewhere private. We have a lot to talk about."

12

FINNIAN CAREFULLY RECOUNTED the events of the past few days to Aidan and Connor, starting with the forest battle. The entire narrative took nearly half an hour. After he had finished, Connor and Aidan were staring at him as though he had lost his mind.

"The prince of Serpenta assassinated?" said Aidan. "And the Aquarians framing Hume for the murder!" He stood up and started pacing. "And now the king of Serpenta wants to have a meeting with us!" He gave a long sigh and shook his head. "I don't even know what to say . . ." He paused for a moment, then exclaimed, "I *knew* those Aquarians were up to something! They acted like friends to our face, then stabbed us in the back!"

Connor nodded and said, "You should have run that lying ambassador straight through with your sword yesterday!" He let out a deep breath and leaned back in his chair. "Well, I suppose this answers the question of why the Serpens invaded Hume in the first place." He leaned toward Finnian. "Under any other circumstances, I would have thought you had lost your mind, but this makes just as much sense as everything else that's happened these past several days." He shook his head. "So much for the Aquarians actually lending us aid." He shifted his focus to Aidan and said, "What are you thinking, my king?"

Aidan stopped pacing and looked at Finnian and said, "You probably know more about the Serpens than anyone else in Hume right now. What do you think are the chances this is just one giant setup?"

Finnian thought for a moment, then replied, "I considered that possibility myself, but I don't think we have much of a choice. Even if you refused to meet with him and took a stand, the armies of the Andruvian Union would be in the fight of their lives. These Serpens are unlike any foe we've ever faced. Using our usual tactics is a wonderful way to get ourselves killed." Finnian paused, then added, "For what it's worth, I feel Zesiro's motives are genuine. When talking with him, I saw a man . . ." He paused again. "Man" wasn't the right word, but it had surely felt like he had been talking with a man. "Well, I saw a *father* who genuinely seemed to be in pain and searching for answers."

Connor asked Finnian, "And he told you we could bring as many soldiers to the meeting as we wanted?"

Finnian nodded. "Yes. He said we could bring our entire army if it would make us feel better."

Connor slapped the table in front of him. "All right, then. I say we take him up on that offer." He looked at Aidan, "Do you agree?"

Aidan nodded. "Absolutely. If they want Hume, we will at least make them work for it!" Connor and Finnian both couldn't help but smile at Aidan's positive attitude, even in times such as this.

Aidan continued, "Finnian, do you have any idea of what military strength the Serpens possess?"

Finnian shook his head and said, "I'm sorry, no. They kept me in a sack every time I was brought outside."

Aidan nodded disappointedly. "We have two days before they arrive. Connor, send word to the remainder of the council in Enlanor. If they are not interested in attending the meeting, fine. I won't ask them to come, but I suspect they're all going to want to attend."

Connor nodded and said, "Very good."

Aidan turned to Finnian. "Get some food and rest. I want you at the meeting with us. Also, I recommend you write a letter to Reagan. We can ensure it will be delivered when the rider travels to Enlanor to talk to the council. She thinks you're dead . . ." Aidan bowed his head. "As did we all." Aidan paused, then continued, "She needs to know you're alive, and you're the best person to tell her."

Aidan smiled and put his hand on Finnian's shoulder. "It's good to have you back, son." He then turned toward the exit and left the tent.

Finnian sat down with a quill and parchment. There was so much he wanted to say, but he thought it best to keep the letter brief. He began to write:

My dearest Reagan,

Yes, I am alive! I was taken captive by the Serpens during the forest battle and was taken to their capital, Tabora. I was released and have just arrived back in Hume, and I am coming home as soon as I am able. I'm so sorry I haven't been able to contact you sooner, but rest assured that I am well and unharmed. Just know for now that during my captivity, I struggled to keep my mind away from you and your beautiful face. I longed to be nowhere other than right next to you, and I count the minutes until I can see you again.

Finnian

Finnian signed the letter and sealed it. Though he promised to return home as soon as possible, he couldn't shake the feeling that it was a promise he wouldn't be able to keep. He had cheated death many times in the past few days. Sooner or later, he knew his luck was bound to run out . . .

Finnian bathed, feasted until he thought his stomach would burst, and was outfitted with a new set of armor and weapons. He would be ready for whatever surprises lay beyond the horizon. He was ready to fight once again, but no longer would he fight for vengeance. He was ready to fight so he could make it home to the woman he loved.

Riders departed from Dunsbury and rode toward Enlanor as quickly as their horses would carry them. After they arrived at the city, they requested an audience with King Amrynn from Elvenna and King Oleg from Dwarvonia.

The kings were delivered the message, and Amrynn read it first. He read about the capture and interrogation of Captain Finnian, the assassination of the Serpentan prince, the supposed plot to frame Hume, and the Serpentan king's request for a meeting.

Oleg could tell from the look on Amrynn's face that whatever was in the letter, it was monumental news. "Well?" he said, feeling impatient.

Amrynn looked up from the letter and said, "Umm . . . You have to read this for yourself."

Oleg snatched the letter from Amrynn's hands and started reading. Several times he looked up from the letter at Amrynn with a confused look.

He finished reading and said, "Is this a joke? Never in my life have I heard of something like this!"

Amrynn nodded and replied, "Nor have I, but it carries the seal of Aidan himself."

"Well, I'm going! There is no chance I am missing this meeting," said Oleg. He gave Amrynn a sly look. "How about you, Elf? Can you muster up the courage to meet the Serpentan king face-to-face?"

Amrynn looked at Oleg and said sarcastically, "Very amusing. Yes, I *think* I can manage it!"

Oleg let out a hearty laugh. "We'll see old friend! We'll see!"

Each left to prepare and mount up for the ordeal that lay ahead. They wanted to arrive in Dunsbury as soon as possible.

The riders carrying the messages then visited the palace to deliver a very special letter to the princess. They gave the letter to the servant positioned at the palace entrance, and he promptly delivered it to Queen Evelyn. The princess had spent her days in her bedroom, refusing to even come down for meals. Evelyn assumed the letter was from Aidan, and she unfolded it and started to read.

Evelyn read the first line of the letter and her legs went weak and she collapsed into the chair behind her. She nearly yelled, "Finnian's alive!" but then covered her mouth with her hand as she continued reading. Tears of joy began streaming down each of her cheeks as she reread the letter.

When she had finished, she folded it back up, both laughing and crying at the same time. She walked up the palace stairs and approached the door to Reagan's bedroom.

She knocked on the door. "Reagan, dear? I have something for you. A letter was just delivered." She waited a long time for an answer, but none came. She knocked again. "Reagan?" Again, there was no answer. "Trust me, you really need to read this letter!"

Evelyn heard stirring on the other side of the door and it finally opened. Reagan's eyes were red and swollen. She had obviously been crying.

Evelyn handed her the letter, and Reagan started to shut the door, but Evelyn put her hand out and stopped it.

"Open it and read it now," Evelyn said.

Reagan gave her mother a confused look and asked, "What does it say?"

"Just read it," replied Evelyn.

Reagan unfolded the letter. Evelyn watched with eager anticipation as Reagan started to read.

Reagan's eyes immediately shot wide open and started to fill with tears, making it difficult to see. She vigorously wiped the tears from her eyes as she continued to read. Evelyn started to laugh softly as Reagan finished the letter and looked up at her. Reagan rushed into her mother's arms and they hugged each other, each shedding tears of joy.

Evelyn finally kissed Reagan on the cheek and said, "It's late. We both need to get some rest." She started walking down the hall toward her own bedroom.

Reagan closed her door and opened the letter again. She couldn't stop reading the letter over and over. After reading it for the final time that night, she carefully folded it and kissed it.

She softly whispered, "Come home to me, Finnian."

13

THE ORCOVAN WARRIORS made their way across Hume toward Enlanor like a plague, destroying everything in their path. They had one goal in mind: Destroy Enlanor. They wanted more land for expansion, and their first target was Hume. When they were successful, the remaining provinces in the Union were to follow. With the help of the Union, Hume had been able to keep them at bay since the beginning of the current Fourth Age, but just barely.

The patrols are typically able to keep the border secure, and if not, they can quickly warn Enlanor of a major attack in time to respond to the threat quickly. However, the Serpentan threat caused most of the patrolling forces to be sent to the south. Any Human patrols the Orcovans did encounter, they killed with swiftness and ease.

The Orcovans began to emerge from the tree line into the open plain where Enlanor rested, and the sight of the capital city on the distant horizon caused the thousands upon thousands of invaders to roar triumphantly.

The soldiers standing watch atop of the high walls began to notice a change in scenery toward the northeastern side of the plains. There was a dark mass far off in the distance, and it didn't take the soldiers long to realize it was a massive army marching toward the capital. They sounded the alarms, and all those on watch raced to the northeast side of the wall and observed as the Orcs drifted closer and closer like a black cloud.

The captain of the watch ran straight to the barracks and reported to his superior. He threw open the office door and exclaimed, "Major! There is a massive force on the northeast horizon marching straight toward Enlanor!"

The major blinked and replied, "I'm sorry, Captain. *What did you say?*"

The captain said again, "There is a huge army marching straight toward us from the northeast!"

The major shot straight up out of his chair and said, "Sound the alarm! Every active and reserve soldier available is to report for duty in full battle dress!" The major covered his face with his hands, then continued, "Over half of our soldiers are deployed to the south. Send riders out as soon as possible and inform the king and the commander!"

The captain left and carried out the major's orders as quickly as he could. The major climbed up to the northeast wall and joined the rest of the soldiers looking out over the plains. All one could see was a dark discoloration on the sweeping yellow horizon, but it was clear to every eye what they were seeing.

He thought to himself, *Why did it have to be now?* He shook his head and started to run back down the spiral staircase within the wall. There was much to prepare for . . .

~

The time for the meeting had come. All members of the council from each province along with Finnian were present and in full battle gear. The reasons for this were twofold: It conveyed the image of power and authority, but more importantly, nobody knew if this discussion would turn into a fight. They wanted to be ready.

The eight thousand Human, Elven, and Dwarven soldiers stood at attention in a large field on the southern edge of Dunsbury. A small portion of this field was once the property of Callum, the first casualty of the Dunsbury attack.

Directly in front of the soldiers was a large tent that had been erected for the meeting. In front of the tent were Finnian and each of the council members mounted on their horses, waiting.

The heat of the sun beat down on them, and there wasn't a single man in armor that didn't have sweat dripping down his face. Everyone sincerely hoped it wouldn't come to fighting today, for the heat was already unbearable.

At midday almost precisely, the council members saw a huge sum of bodies appear over the crest of a large hill in the distance. All of the members of the council were seasoned veterans of war, but they each shuddered in their armor when they saw the horde of Serpens appear over the hill.

Their numbers were more than what was expected, at least twenty thousand warriors, by Aidan's estimate. Furthermore, the Serpens had brought trebuchets and siege towers.

Connor leaned toward Aidan and said, "They're ready to destroy an entire city."

Aidan nodded and replied, "Let's just hope it's their contingency plan and nothing else."

Amrynn and Oleg looked at one another and then at Aidan. Oleg said, "They must have brought their entire army!"

The Serpen trebuchets were quite impressive. They were much larger than any they had ever seen, and looked capable of slinging enormous projectiles that would have no difficulty pulverizing even the strongest of walls. They were pulled by large, elephant-like animals covered in thick, tan fur that protected them from the intense sun rays of the Serpentan desert. They had a short, broad trunk with large tusks that grew outwardly from just below their large eyes. They were unlike any animal the council members had ever seen. None of them were aware these animals even existed and therefore had no name for them in the common Andruvian language.

Amrynn said out loud to the whole group, "Has anyone else ever seen these animals before?"

Everyone in the group shook their heads.

Connor replied, "They must live further south in the Serpentan Desert. After all, we don't even know how far south the desert goes or what lies beyond it."

Oleg snorted and said facetiously, "Why don't you ask them when they get here? Maybe they'll take us on a guided tour!"

"Gentlemen, let's stay focused," said Aidan.

Besides the siege weapons, all of the Serpen forces were infantry. Serpens do not use any form of cavalry. Their snakelike bodies aren't able to ride animals like horses, nor do they need to. They are capable of moving at speeds much faster than Humans, and though they are slower than horses on solid ground, they are easily faster when on sand.

The mass of Serpens approached the council members and stopped just in front of them. Each of the council members had the same first impression of the Serpens: They're nightmarish. Their size, the way they move, the unsettling gaze of their eyes . . . No one could prepare oneself to come face-to-face with them.

The front line began to part, and four high-ranking Serpens emerged from the group. All but one of them carried a spear and shield, and all four of them had metal bands around their necks, signifying them as high-ranking officials in the Serpentan army. Two of them wore a bronze band. The third Serpen was High Commander Adisa wearing a silver band. The fourth, who was leading the other three, carried himself with much dignity and wore an ornate gold necklace. This was King Zesiro.

Aidan looked at Finnian and motioned for him to follow, and the three kings from the council rode forward on their horses and met the group of Serpens. The two parties halted and stared at one another for a moment, then Aidan spoke.

"Greetings. I am King Aidan of Hume," he said.

Amrynn was the second to speak. The Serpens' eyes shifted to him as he said, "I am Amrynn, king of Elvenna."

Oleg finally introduced himself. "I am King Oleg of Dwarvonia."

The council members shuddered at the sinister appearance of these creatures' penetrating stare.

Aidan pointed at Finnian. "And this is Captain Finnian, with whom I understand you are already acquainted."

Surprised, Zesiro looked at Finnian and he recognized him as soon as he more closely studied his face. He felt some semblance of shame at his inability to recognize the one he had spent time interrogating just a couple of days prior.

He slithered forward some and said in a raspy voice, "Greetings, kings. I am Zesiro, king of Serpenta." He motioned to Adisa. "This is Adisa, the high commander of the Serpentan Army." Adisa bowed his head. Then Zesiro pointed at the two remaining Serpens with the bronze bands, saying, "And this is Bahati and Isabis, my two petty commanders. The three of them are my top and most trusted officers." Bahati and Isabis bowed their heads in unison.

All of the council members noticed the thick accent Zesiro had and his apparent difficulty forming the words of the common Andruvian language. If one did not listen carefully, it would be difficult to understand him.

Zesiro continued, "I did not expect the kings from Elvenna and Dwarvonia to be present. It is a welcome surprise."

Amrynn and Oleg exchanged a brief glance with one another, almost as if to say, "What did he mean by that?" It was difficult to tell from Zesiro's inflections whether there was a hint of malice in his voice or not.

Aidan motioned toward the tent behind him. "This tent was built specifically for this meeting. Shall we get started?"

"Certainly," said Zesiro, and all four Serpens slithered over to the tent. Aidan and Connor each opened a flap to the entrance and first the Serpens entered, then the Elven and Dwarven council members. Aidan, Connor, and Finnian followed and closed the flaps behind them.

⁓

At the time the Serpens and the council members entered the tent, riders from Enlanor were arriving in Dunsbury with an urgent message . . .

⁓

Finnian and the council members sat on one side of a table that had been set up in the center of the tent, and the Serpens approached the opposite side of the table. Chairs were set up, but because they are unable to sit in chairs, they shoved them aside. They coiled their long bodies underneath them, creating a makeshift chair with their bodies and stood erect at the edge of the table.

Zesiro did not waste any time starting the discussion. He began by asking, "Why did I call this meeting?"

The council members were a little perplexed. Zesiro's question did not seem rhetorical. It appeared he was waiting for them to answer.

There was silence for several seconds until Aidan finally said, "Forgive me, but I am not sure I understand."

Zesiro looked at him and said, "I want you to tell me why it was necessary for me to call this meeting. *Why* am I here?"

Aidan understood. The Serpentan king wanted to see what they would confess to before they got to the main topic at hand. *He wants to see how much we know and how we handle this whole situation*, he thought. Aidan thought it best to be completely transparent and empathetic.

He brought his hands to the table, clasped them, and said, "King Zesiro, Captain Finnian has updated all of us regarding your situation. First of all, please accept our deepest condolences for the loss of your son. When every one of us heard the news of the assassination, we were appalled." The remainder of the council began nodding their heads. "We all have sons ourselves, and I can personally guarantee that each of us would be inconsolable if something were to happen to them."

Zesiro looked down at the ground for a second, then looked back up at Aidan. At that moment, Aidan hoped he hadn't inadvertently caused tension to arise by mentioning the death of Zesiro's son, Dakiri.

He continued, "Please understand, King, that the Andruvian Union had absolutely nothing to do with it. Above all, we desire peace for our provinces, and there would be no benefit for us to carry out a heinous act such as this. This was not an act of war. Killing an innocent child is simply murder. Relations between Hume and Aquaria have been sour ever since the war at the end of the First Age, and based upon what Captain Finnian told me he learned during his captivity, it would seem they are trying to start a war between the Andruvian Union and Serpenta and reap the spoils: our land."

Zesiro surveyed each of the faces across the table from him. Even now, he had trouble differentiating between the different races, save for the Dwarves. The only discernible difference he could confidently identify was the difference in height and the fact that Dwarves have a very brawny build.

Zesiro began, "As I look at all your faces, I must confess that I have difficulty telling your races apart." He looked at Finnian and said, "I didn't even recognize you until your king introduced you, Captain."

Every one of the council members was holding their breath. They still couldn't predict whether this meeting was headed toward peace or war.

Zesiro continued, "The history of the Andruvian Union is not well known by our people, and that is mostly due to apathy. Yet still, we are somewhat aware of the ill relations between the Humans and the Aquarians because we have witnessed hostilities between the two over the years."

Aidan and Connor looked at each other questioningly. Zesiro noticed the look and responded, "My warriors are quite skilled at remaining unseen when they want to be. Forgive us for our intrusion, but I can assure you all that the surveillance was only in the interest of security."

The council members all looked at one another. Oleg turned to Zesiro and said, "Are you admitting to violating our borders and spying on us!"

Amrynn quickly rebuked him, saying, "Oleg! How is it any different from what we've tried to do with their border? The only difference is that they are stealthy enough not to be seen. Besides, they've never even attacked us!" Amrynn paused, then added, "Well . . . until now, anyway."

It was true that every province in the Union attempted to scout out Serpenta, but the attempts were typically a disaster. The scouts were usually discovered and promptly killed by Serpens guarding the border.

Oleg sighed loudly. He raised his hands and said to Zesiro, "My apologies. Please, continue."

Zesiro hardly seemed fazed by Oleg's outburst. He continued, "As I was saying, I was foolish and did not mandate the Aquarian border be watched nearly as closely. We thought them feeble and not much of a threat to our province."

Zesiro uncoiled himself and began to slowly slither back and forth in the tent, similar to how a Human would pace back and forth. Finnian noticed that the Serpen king had a habit of doing that, for he had done it many times during the interrogations.

Zesiro continued, "After speaking with Captain Finnian, it was obvious to all of us . . ." Zesiro motioned to the other Serpens. "That the assassins are a different race from the rest of the eight captives from the battle." Zesiro paused and decided to add, "They are all well and will be released back to you unharmed."

Every one of the council members breathed a sigh of relief, both for the reassurance that they were not being blamed for the assassination and that the prisoners were unharmed.

Zesiro continued, "There is no denying that every one of the assassins are Aquarians. Therefore, please accept my deepest apology for the many deaths of your people over these past days. Their blood, my own soldiers' blood, and . . ." Zesiro stopped for several seconds, mustering up the strength to continue speaking. "And the blood of my son, Dakiri, is on the hands of the Aquarians."

Aidan stood up from the table and said, "On behalf of the Union, we thank you for your understanding." He did this mainly because he knew of Oleg's impulsiveness and wanted to just accept Zesiro's apology rather than having an argument start over all the dead Union soldiers. There would certainly be no benefit to that.

Oleg shifted anxiously in his seat, but he kept his silence.

Aidan continued, "And regarding the Aquarians, I can assure you that their crimes will not go unpunished . . ."

Zesiro cut Aidan off and said sternly, "You are absolutely correct! But their punishment is not *yours* to give! I will personally ensure they pay for the death of your soldiers and my son. Of that, you have my word!"

Aidan nodded and didn't argue. He couldn't blame the Serpen king's insistence to be the one to make the Aquarians pay. This was personal, and he imagined he would feel the same way should their positions be reversed. Furthermore, it certainly made things easier for the Union. If the Serpens wanted to be the ones to take the fight to Aquaria, they were more than welcome.

Oleg cleared his throat. "If I may, I have one question for you, King Zesiro."

Zesiro stared at Oleg, waiting for the question.

"What lies south of the Serpentan Desert? It has been a mystery to all our people for ages," asked Oleg.

Aidan shot Oleg a foul look. His question was hardly on topic, and this wasn't the time or the place for idle discussion.

Upon hearing Oleg's question, the four Serpens gave one another an apprehensive look.

Zesiro finally answered, "The terrible jungles of Avia. Home of the Avians, or as our people call them . . ." Zesiro uttered a sequence of hisses and snarls. "In Andruvian, this means, 'sky hunters.'"

Everyone in the room blankly stared at Zesiro. The ancient stories of the "bird people" were true, and each of them had at least ten follow-up questions. Even Aidan was now curious to learn more.

News of the Orcovans spotted marching toward Enlanor was reported to the officers outside the tent, and they started to panic. The Orcs had likely reached the city by the time the riders were able to report the news, and the longer they waited, more people were likely to die. Majority of Hume's forces were in Dunsbury, and those who were left in Enlanor would not last long against that army of Orcs.

The officers debated whether they should interrupt the meeting to deliver the news to Aidan. The soldiers noticed that the officers were visibly anxious about something unknown to them, which in turn made them anxious. The officers eventually decided this news was too urgent to wait for the meeting to end.

Zesiro had just finished insisting that the Serpens be the one to deal with the Aquarians when there was a knock on the door of the tent.

Feeling irritated, Aidan called out, "Yes? This had better be important."

One of the officers came through the door of the tent and stepped inside. When the council saw the concerned look on his face, they concluded that news was worth the interruption. Even the Serpens could discern the look on his face indicated there was an emergency.

The officer said, "Forgive me for the intrusion, but riders just arrived from Enlanor. Orcovans are marching on to the city."

Oleg and Amrynn immediately stood up from their chairs with horrified looks on their faces.

"How many?" asked Aidan.

"Uncertain. At least ten thousand, but probably more," said the officer.

Aidan buried his face in his hands. He looked at the council members, then at the Serpens. "I am so very sorry, but the capital of Hume is probably under siege by Orcs as we speak, and most of our forces are here in Dunsbury. We have to leave *now*."

The council members began to quietly deliberate, and Zesiro turned to his officers and started issuing orders in their native language. The hisses and snarls caught the attention of the others, and they waited until the discussion was finished. They worried that the interruption of the meeting had offended the Serpens.

Zesiro finished addressing his officers, and each of them bowed and hissed a short response. Zesiro turned toward the council and said, "We are sorry to hear of your predicament. Our people have never encountered Orcovans in the past, but Captain Finnian has informed me that you have been at war with them for quite some time. Is this correct?"

Aidan replied, "Yes, King. The combined strength of each of our provinces is barely enough to stand against them. Without the immediate return of our soldiers, the Human capital will be destroyed . . . along with my family."

Zesiro nodded. "Go. Protect your homeland, and . . . protect your family." Zesiro paused for emphasis. They all felt the weight of his words, the words of a father who had just lost his child. Zesiro continued, "I have arranged for five thousand of our own warriors to accompany you. After all, this meeting I called is the reason that your forces are not present to protect your capital in the first place. Consider it a peace offering."

Aidan couldn't believe his ears! "Forgive me, King. Did you say you were sending five thousand of your own warriors to help defend our capital?"

"That is correct. I have already made the arrangements." Zesiro motioned to one of the Serpens behind him. "Adisa, my high commander, has volunteered to lead our warriors. He will personally see to it that they defend your capital as if it were their own." Adisa slithered forward and made a slight bow to Aidan.

"Now go. Defend your homeland and protect your families. I have matters to attend to with our neighbors in Aquaria," said Zesiro maliciously.

Aidan bowed very low and said, "You have the deepest gratitude of Hume, and we are indebted to you." He rose back up. "So there will be peace between our provinces once again?"

"Respect our border, and we will respect yours. You have my word that the Serpens will no longer cross your border." He looked at Oleg and Amrynn. "You *all* have my word."

Zesiro turned to Aidan and said, "Good luck, king of Hume." He gave a slight bow of the head, then turned to Oleg and Amrynn. "And to the rest of you, good luck." He bowed once more, then left the tent. All Serpens except Adisa followed him.

The remaining Serpen approached Aidan and said, "My warriors are ready and at your disposal, king of Hume. I can guarantee you they will be eager to fight. We Serpens have never met Orcovans in battle, and we always relish a new challenge."

Aidan bowed slightly and replied, "Yes, thank you, High Commander. We will be leaving for Enlanor as soon as possible. Have your warriors ready to leave. And again, all of Hume thanks you."

Adisa looked Aidan in the eye, which gave Aidan a slight chill, and he said, "King of Hume, listen to me. We are warriors. Your soldiers are not like ours. We were raised for this purpose. Our only family is our brothers with which we fight alongside. We have no other calling in life than to fight for, and if necessary, die for our king, Zesiro. And our king has given us the order and the *privilege* of fighting a new enemy alongside new allies. Nothing would make us happier. *Do not* thank me again."

Everyone in the room was taken aback. There was a cultural chasm between these races, and Aidan was inadvertently offending the Serpens who saw it as not only an honor to fight, but the very reason they even existed. To insinuate that their assistance was obligatory actually demeaned them. To Serpen warriors, fighting was as natural and as eating.

Aidan, Oleg, and Amrynn each nodded with humility, and the group quickly discussed the travel arrangements around the table. They finished in only a matter of minutes, then they each left the tent to mobilize their soldiers.

Before leaving, Adisa addressed his Serpen warriors in their native tongue. Their reaction seemed to be that of a tiger being unleashed upon its prey. Aidan was struck by their genuine excitement, and it only solidified Adisa's rebuke in the tent. They had been raised for one purpose: fighting. Their life revolved around their military training until they were deemed unfit for service and subsequently released to pursue a life of marriage and child-bearing. Not only would they get to unleash the skills they had spent their lives honing, they would be unleashing it on a foe they've never encountered before. Nothing would have excited them more.

The Humans, Elves, Dwarves, and Serpens all departed Dunsbury as one, massive fighting force bound for Enlanor. Aidan, Connor, and Finnian led the pack with the Serpens directly behind them. The remainder of the Human, Elven, and Dwarven soldiers followed the five thousand Serpens: a multiracial horde riding with zeal and vigor and ready for battle. They moved as quickly as they were able, riding through the evening and the night, hoping and praying they would arrive in time.

Finnian thought of Reagan. His mind conjured up images of her in the bunkers, terrified and crying. These mental images fueled his rage and determination. The Orcs had already taken his mother and father away from him, they would *not* take her away as well! It was time for their campaign of terror against Hume to end! He gritted his teeth and gripped the reins as tightly as he could. He looked to his left saw Aidan and Connor riding with the same looks of determination on their faces. They all had loved ones in Enlanor they needed to protect. Aidan glanced over at him briefly, then focused forward again.

Aidan's emotions were mutual. He thought constantly of his wife and children. He had fought the Orcovans for most of his life, and he was not going to let them harm any more of his people. He now had help from his new Serpen allies. He had not seen them in action yet, but he had heard the eyewitness accounts of the fury they can unleash upon their enemies. He looked forward to witnessing that same fury being unleashed onto the Orcs.

Kieran rode along with the masses, and for the first time in his military career, he had no apprehension about charging into battle. He glanced ahead and saw the Serpens, and he actually felt excitement. He had faced them twice now, and no longer would he have to stare down their dreaded spears pointed at him. It was now the Orcs' turn, and with that thought, a smile formed across his face. He was ready.

14

EVERY MILITARY-AGE MAN in Enlanor was in full battle dress, watching from the city walls as fifteen thousand Orcovans marched in formation toward them. Many were purging the contents of their stomachs out of nervousness as they watched the antagonists approach. There wasn't a man present who didn't feel as though his heart would beat right out of his chest. There was little else for them to do than to watch and prepare for whatever fate awaited them.

The rest of the city's population took refuge in Enlanor's extensive network of underground bunkers. When the Orcovan trebuchets unleashed their projectiles, there wouldn't be a single safe location above ground.

Women, children, and the elderly huddled together, each trying to console one another. All who had the misfortune of catching a glance of the advancing throng of Orcovan warriors knew there was no hope of salvation from their bloodlust, not without the rest of the Human army.

Evelyn, Reagan, and Owen were among the masses in the bunkers. Owen had wanted to fight, but being only seventeen, he had no training and was too young to be allowed to fight. Of course, an exception would have undoubtedly been made had he had any military training given the current circumstances. Evelyn and Reagan embraced one another, almost shaking, for they knew that all the military might Hume could muster would *still* not be enough.

When the Orcovan trebuchets were in range, their advance on the city halted. They blasted their ominous battle horns, and they all triumphantly roared. The sound was almost deafening for the soldiers on the city walls. As the thunderous sound subsided, the trebuchets unleashed a rain of boulders.

At the same time, the catapults within the city returned fire. Their primary targets were the trebuchets. If the trebuchets could be disabled, the Orcs would have to resort to rushing and assaulting the gate and drawbridge. The Orc siege towers were unable to get close enough to the walls due to the moat which surrounded the city. A direct assault on the gate and drawbridge was the last resort for the attackers, for it would put them within range of the Human archers.

The boulders from the Orcovan trebuchets crashed down onto the city, piercing large holes into the buildings. The city wall was hit by several boulders, but its construction was sturdy enough to withstand the barrage . . . for now. It was only a matter of time before the wall took too much damage and crumpled, giving the Orcovan infantry an avenue to flood into the city. Once this happened, it would be the beginning of the end for Enlanor. They simply didn't have enough men.

The projectiles from the Human catapults rained down upon the attackers, killing groups of warriors at a time. One of the trebuchets suffered a direct hit and was destroyed beyond repair, but the Orcs had plenty to spare. There were screams and whimpers among the crowds in the bunkers every time an Orcovan boulder was heard crashing into the city. Had they not known better, it almost sounded like a furious thunderstorm above.

The back and forth of the artilleries exchanging their payloads continued. The casualties of the Humans were minimal thus far. The only fatalities occurred when a boulder landed directly onto the walkway on the wall, crushing the unfortunate soldiers.

As night began to fall, the soldiers were growing weary. There was still very little for them to do. Most could only stand and watch hopelessly as their buildings and homes were destroyed.

The night was long and arduous for the Human soldiers. Visibility was low, and they had to constantly listen to the ominous sound of trebuchets releasing their boulders and hope they didn't land directly on top of them.

Roughly half of the Orcovan trebuchets had been destroyed, but many of the Human catapults had been destroyed as well. Furthermore, certain sections of the wall were severely damaged, and the soldiers were getting nervous that they would crumble down with every next boulder that was launched at the city. A portion of the soldiers were stationed behind the crippled portions of the wall, ready to fight should a hole be made.

As the sun rose in the morning, the soldiers could again look out over the field, and their already-dwindling spirits continued to drop. They had barely even put a dent in the Orc population.

One of the remaining Orc trebuchets slung a boulder that smashed directly into a weakened section of the wall and it crumbled. The wall was compromised!

The soldiers began screaming alarms to one another, and everyone available rushed to the area to defend the break in the wall.

The Orc horns blasted again, and the warriors charged toward the wall. While the siege weapons were not able to cross the moat, the foot soldiers could, but with some difficulty. It didn't take long for them to be within range of the Human archers, and they began firing volley after volley at the charging attackers. Orc warriors fell intermittently as the arrows rained down, but they were too well armored for the archers to be terribly effective.

The Orcs eventually reached the breach in the wall. The soldiers defending the broken wall had the idea to position the crossbow-like ballistas directly in front of the opening, and they opened fire as the Orcs started emerging through the hole.

It was not what the ballistas were designed for, but it was effective. As a group of Orcs came through the small opening, one of the ballistas would release its large spear and pulverized the attackers. No amount of heavy Orcovan armor would protect against a projectile of that size. The Human soldiers would then reload the ballista as another one unleashed its payload into the next group. The remaining Orcovans that were not killed by the ballistas were felled by archers positioned behind the opening and on top of the wall.

The strategy was working, but the ammunition for the ballistas was quickly diminishing. The soldiers readied their shields and spears as they prepared for the inevitable flood of invaders.

Suddenly, they heard the Orcovan horns sounds once again, but rather than a single, long blast, they heard three short blasts. Those who had been attacking the breach in the wall halted their assault and regrouped with the rest of the Orcs beyond the wall.

The defenders looked at each other in confusion. The soldiers on top of the wall did the same. Many were asking, "What are they doing?" The Orcs were strangely repositioning themselves facing toward the south. All the Human soldiers looked to see what had captured the Orcs' attention, and they saw a huge sum of soldiers emerging over the crest of the hill in the distance.

In unison, they all raised their weapons into the air and shouted and screamed in excitement! At the top of their lungs, they exclaimed, *"They're here! They're here!"*

There was a thunderous harmony of horns that sounded from the army of reinforcements: horns of Hume, horns of Elvenna, horns of Dwarvonia, and a fourth group of horns they didn't recognize.

The horde on the hill continued blasting their horns, and the defenders of the city answered with their own. The Orcs continued to regroup into their formations and awaited the onslaught of these new reinforcements.

~

Aidan, Connor, and Finnian sat on their horses on the crest of the hill, and Adisa stood next to them. Oleg and Amrynn sat on their mounts, each in front of their own group of soldiers. Aidan, Connor, and Finnian surveyed the scene in front of them. Under any other circumstances, they would have been horrified at the multitude of Orcs attacking the city, but nothing would spoil their confidence today. Today, they had deadly new allies fighting at their side, and they would not accept any outcome other than victory.

Aidan drew his sword, raised it high, and let out his most fearsome battle cry. The rest of the forces joined in, roaring triumphantly. The energy was infectious. One couldn't help but feel the surge of excitement and adrenaline.

Adisa approached Aidan and said, "Let my warriors lead the charge." Aidan was about to protest, but something about the confidence of the Serpens voice made him think otherwise.

"Make sure you leave some for the rest of us!" he replied.

Adisa let out a sinister hissing sound and nodded in acknowledgment. He slithered over to his officers and began giving orders in their Serpentan language.

Aidan, Connor, and Finnian watched as the orders were relayed throughout their ranks. After the orders had been issued, the Serpens performed their typical pre-battle ritual: They turned to their fellow warriors on each side and touched their foreheads together while resting their right hands on the back of their partner's head. It was their way of honoring one another should some of them not survive. As far as Serpen warriors are concerned, every other warrior is their brother. They have no connection with their biological family, and their brothers-in-arms are the only family they have.

Finnian gained a whole new level of appreciation for this snakelike race. He admired their camaraderie and respect for one another. Though they had an intimidating, vexing exterior, they truly were an honorable and inspiring people.

Adisa turned to Aidan and said, "Good luck, king of Hume."

Aidan responded, "Good luck to you, High Commander."

Adisa turned to Finnian and said, "Though we started as enemies, today we fight as allies! Good luck, Captain."

Finnian bowed and said, "It is an honor to fight next to you, High Commander."

Adisa positioned himself in front of his warriors, raised his spear to the sky, and let out a long, bone-chilling howl, and the rest of the Serpens joined in.

The veterans of the forest battle immediately recognized this howl. It was the same sound they had all heard as they were charging into the forest. Unbeknownst to them, this howl was actually a phrase in the Serpen language. Loosely translated, they were yelling, *"As one, until death!"* This, too, was a pre-battle ritual of the Serpens.

As the howl came to an end, the Serpens began their charge down the hill toward the Orcovan line.

After the Serpens started down the hill, Aidan ordered the charge. The Human, Elven, and Dwarven horns sounded, and the three groups proceeded to charge in unison down the hill behind the Serpens.

The Serpen spearmen were in the front, and the archers were in the rear. Because they ambulate by slithering, they are able to release their arrows accurately even while traveling at their maximum speed. This makes Serpen archers devastating on an open battlefield. They will never stop moving and continue to sling arrows onto their opponents from a distance.

As the Serpens made their way down the hill, the archers continuously shot arrows into the Orcovans. The Orcovan front line held their shields to the front with spears extended, and the lines behind them would hold their shield over their heads to prevent arcing arrows from falling on top of them.

These tactics proved to be effective against their usual enemies; however, they were not as effective against the Serpens. The archers would not arc their arrows from afar like the Union archers would. They shot them straight into the shields and the armored legs of the front line during the charge, causing the Orcovans to hide behind the shields and not be readily able to watch what was happening in front of them. As a result, the front line was less prepared for the clash. When the two lines did clash, the Serpens could easily avoid the spears by employing their classic tactic of striking forward with lightning speed and thrusting their spear at a vulnerable area of their target.

The Orcovan archers returned fire at the charging forces, but the Serpens were able to reach the front line with only mild casualties due to their speed, fast reflexes, and expert manipulation of their large tower shields.

It was now obvious to Aidan and all the rest why Adisa insisted that the Serpens lead the charge. Their tactics and mobile archers softened the Orcovan defenses to minimize casualties for the Union cavalry.

When the Serpens were within twenty feet of the Orcs, they struck forward with their spears, decimating their front line. None of the forest battle veterans were surprised, but the rest of the soldiers were startled by the deadly speed these snakelike people had. Orcs in the front line were already toppling to the ground before they even realized what had happened.

Finnian watched the Serpens carry out their assault, and he couldn't help but laugh. He had been on the receiving end of the Serpen attacks, and he did not envy the Orcs at this moment. He knew what they were likely feeling at this instant: confusion, fear, and defenselessness against this strange new enemy.

Hundreds of Orcs were dead in the blink of an eye as the Serpen spears pierced right through the openings in their helms. Those directly behind the front line were completely caught off guard. They had never encounter tactics like these before, and before they could react, they, too, died in a similar fashion.

To make matters worse for the Orcs, their shield wall was now decimated, making them even more susceptible to the Serpen archers. Their armor was heavy enough to repel the arrows, but they had to keep their shields raised which limited their vision, and thus, their readiness for the strikes of the Serpen spearmen.

The largest threat the Orcs posed to the Serpens were their archers. Though they were masters at manipulating their shields, one could only do so much against barrages of arrows.

The Union forces reached the Orcovans only moments later. They had suffered heavy casualties during the charge, for they were not able to protect themselves or their horses from arrows as well as the Serpens. Hundreds of Humans, Elves, Dwarves, and horses littered the large hill.

After reaching the Orcovan line, however, the cavalry was able to slice right into the defenders like a hot knife into butter. Much to their chagrin, the Orcs had a quite small cavalry. Their homeland and climate was not conducive to breeding and raising horses as well as Hume, and since they were not part of the Andruvian Union, trading with Hume to obtain more horses was obviously not an option. It was because of this precise reason the Orcs wanted to conquer Hume first. They knew the value of horses in battle, and they wanted to bolster their number of cavalry before continuing their conquest.

Finnian rode into the Orcovan line using his spear like a lance. He struck an Orc's breastplate, making it glance upward and pierce directly into the neck of the warrior. The spear landed hard enough that it was yanked clean from his grip and he was forced to leave it behind and draw his hand-and-a-half sword.

Kieran had never been in a proper charge before. He held his spear as steady as he could and waited for the clash. He slammed into the Orcovan line with the rest of the soldiers, and though his spear did not hit its mark, he felt a wave of exhilaration. The flood of cavalry was overwhelming the Orcs. In all the excitement, he yelled as loud as he could in a shout of triumph.

Aidan and Connor held back from the front and directed the officers as the battle played out. They were both extremely pleased with the ease at which the cavalry was able to penetrate the Orc defenses. Never had they seen their line break so easily.

Connor looked and Aidan and said, "This is incredible!"

Aidan simply laughed in reply.

The soldiers in the city watched the success of the charge and cheered loudly. It quickly became apparent to them that not only were Union soldiers on the field, but Serpens as well! Nobody knew what to think, but as long as they kept killing Orcs, they'd keep cheering.

A portion of the soldiers guarding the city were ordered to charge the Orcs from the west side and flank them. They rushed out onto the field to hit the Orcs as hard as they could, though many tried to keep their distance from the Serpens just as a precaution.

Though they had superior numbers, the Orcovan officers watched these events unfold and started to panic. They had never seen warriors like the Serpens, and they had no idea how to fight them. Their usual tactics weren't working. They would have to adapt if they were going to survive this fight. Their archers were clearly the most valuable warriors on the field against the Serpens, so they started to relay orders for the warriors with pole arms to focus on protecting the archers. However, this strategy was quickly abandoned because it made these clusters of Orcs better targets for charging Union cavalry. The battlefield was pandemonium, and they were running out of ideas.

As the battle progressed, more and more members of the cavalry started fighting on foot, for their mounts were getting injured or killed.

Finnian had thus far managed to stay on his horse. He charged into a group of three Orcs, slashing at their backs as they were engaging a Serpen. He knew there was little he could do against their armor with his sword, but he was more so interested in distracting them to give the Serpen a better opening to attack.

He slammed his sword off the helm of one of the Orcs, disorienting him. The Serpen wasted no idea to capitalize on this opportunity. He lunged forward and stabbed his spear straight into the Orcovan's shoulder, finding its way through a joint in the armor. Finnian saw the tip of the spear protrude out the back of the shoulder, and the Orc howled in pain.

Finnian turned his gaze forward again just in time to realize he was riding directly into the spear of another Orc. The spear sunk deeply into the horse's chest and it crumbled to the ground, throwing Finnian forward several feet.

He rolled once and scrambled to his feet, still holding his sword. He got to his feet just in time. The Orc who wielded the spear was charging toward him with his sword drawn. Finnian has lost his shield, so he raised his sword into a defensive position. It was in swordplay that he was the most confident, but he still had to concentrate. Orcs are much stronger than Humans, which is a substantial advantage in a sword fight.

The Orc swung his heavy sword diagonally down from the right side, and Finnian parried and sidestepped to the right. He swung his sword around and brought it down onto the Orc's shoulder, and it bounced off his armor. Finnian brought his sword back into the defensive position and studied the body language of his opponent. He only needed to be patient and wait for a window to counterattack.

The Orc thrust his sword toward Finnian's abdomen, but he telegraphed the sword thrust too much. Finnian was ready for it. He quickly jumped to the left and lunged forward, swinging his sword around and slamming the less-protected back of the Orc's right knee. The knee buckled immediately, and the Orc hustled to rise back to a standing position, but he wasn't fast enough. Finnian drew his sword back and thrust it down between the Orc's helm and back plate. The sword sank deep into the Orc's thorax, and death was almost instantaneous.

Finnian had some trouble withdrawing his sword out of the Orc's back. He tugged on it, but it was pinched between the Orc's plates of armor. Just then, he noticed out of the corner of his eye that another Orc was rushing toward him with his poleaxe poised to strike. Finnian didn't have time. He let go of the hilt of his own sword and rolled forward, grabbing the dead Orc's sword off the ground as he did so. He had dived just in time, for the second Orc's poleaxe crashed into the ground where Finnian had been standing a split second ago. Finnian came to a standing position and held this new sword in a guard position. It was heavier than he was used to, but it was still very wieldable if he used two hands. He had a momentary thought of how good the sword felt in his hands. It was comfortable and well-balanced.

Just like the stereotype that Orcovans were merely dumb brutes, many Humans considered Orc weapons and armor to be inferior to the smithing techniques the Union weapon and armor smiths used. In reality, the Orcovans used smithing techniques that were comparable to the rest of the races and made very fine weapons and armor.

Finnian's heart was pounding in his chest. There was little he could do with a sword against a poleaxe. The Orc had greater reach and power. The Orc was pointing his weapon straight toward Finnian. Finnian stared straight into the point of the spear tip and tried to keep his distance. His only hope would be to dodge a thrust and quickly close the distance so the poleaxe wouldn't be effective.

The Orc thrust the spear tip forward with power and precision, and Finnian didn't evade the thrust quickly enough. The spear tip rammed into his shoulder plate, glancing off to the side. Though it didn't injure Finnian, it knocked him off balance and he stumbled backward.

The Orc stepped forward and delivered a second thrust that buried into Finnian's chest plate. Because he had already been stumbling backward, his momentum took some of the power out of the thrust, and it only pierced one inch into his armor. The strike threw Finnian to the ground, and he felt pressure and pain where the spear tip punctured his armor. The tip had punctured his skin, but not deep enough to enter his chest cavity.

Finnian laid on his back gasping for air because he had had his breath knocked out of him. The Orc rushed toward him while drawing his dagger to finish Finnian off, but just as the Orc reached him, a sword tip burst through the front of his neck. The Orc's blood spilled out onto Finnian and he crumpled to the ground. Finnian looked up, and standing before him was Kieran.

The scene before him was very familiar. Finnian had saved the lives of the royal family in a similar series of events four years ago.

Kieran bent over, grabbed Finnian by the hand, and said, "Come on, Captain!" He brought Finnian to his feet and pointed at the hole in his chest plate. "Are you hurt?"

Finnian coughed as he finally recovered his breath and said, "No, no, I'm fine."

Kieran nodded once, then ran off to the nearest Orc to continue fighting.

Finnian watched him leave and said under his breath, "Thank you." He bent over and picked up the Orcovan sword laying on the ground. He inspected it for a second, then shook his head and dropped it back onto the ground. He rushed over to the other dead Orc and pried his own sword from the body. He looked for and spotted Kieran in the midst of the fighting and ran toward him. He figured he owed it to him to look after him now.

Thanks to the Serpens, the battle was still heavily favoring the Union. The Orcs were too occupied trying to counter their attacks that they barely had time to pay attention to the rest of the Union soldiers. They quickly learned that if they turned their back on a Serpen for even a second, they would get skewered by an expertly placed spear thrust.

The acrobatic Elves danced with their dual sabers and the burly Dwarves hacked and slashed with their halberds. Though the Orcovan numbers continually dwindled, the Union forces were still taking heavy losses. The power of the Orcs' bows was devastating, even when you wore plate armor. The Orcs designed their arrowheads specifically for piercing, and the only piece of equipment that would reliably stop them was a shield. Armor that could withstand their armor-piercing arrows was simply too heavy and slowed down its wearer.

Adisa engaged a foursome of Orcs that were fighting back to back. They used their shields to create a protective box around them, and they would jab at enemies with the spear tip of their poleaxes.

Adisa bent over and picked up an Orcovan spear that was lying on the ground and threw it directly at one of the Orcs. The spear embedded in his shield, making the Orc flinch. It was the opening Adisa was hoping for. He shot forward and slammed his weight into the stumbling Orc's shield, and he toppled over. Adisa recoiled and shot forward again, this time thrusting his own spear directly into the back of the neck of the Orc facing the opposite direction. The Orc crumbled in a heap.

One of the other two still standing turned around to see what had happened, but before he could react, Adisa struck again and thrust his spear into the opening of the Orc's faceplate. Adisa withdrew the spear from the Orc's skull and quickly wrapped his arm around the helm of the only Orc left on his feet and stabbed the spear head into the side of his neck.

The only Orc left of the foursome was still on the ground, trying to get up. He managed to draw his sword, and he thrust it upward into Adisa's abdomen.

Adisa roared in pain as he pulled his spear head out of the previous Orc's neck. He curled his tail around, wrapped it around the Orc's sword arm, and withdrew the sword from his abdomen, wincing in pain as he did.

He bent down and looked the terrified Orc directly in the eyes. Adisa let out a monstrous snarl and plunged the spear straight down through the opening in his faceplate.

Adisa held his hand to his abdominal wound. He looked down and saw that his hand was covered in bright red blood. Another Serpen saw him holding his bloody wound and called out, "Commander! How badly are you wounded?"

Adisa looked at him and said, "I'm fi—"

Just then, an Orcovan arrow shot straight through Adisa's neck and continued on its trajectory. Blood poured from each side of his neck as he fell to the ground.

The other Serpen yelled, "Commander!" and quickly slithered over to Adisa. He slid his hand underneath Adisa's head and turned his face toward his. Adisa's eyes darted back and forth and he moved his mouth, but no sound came. Saying nothing, the two stared at one another until Adisa's pupils suddenly dilated and his eyes rolled into the back of his head. Adisa was gone.

The Serpen brought Adisa's forehead to his own and quietly said, "Farewell, brother." He carefully laid the head back down. He dropped his own spear, picked up Adisa's, and continued the fight with renewed vigor. He would ensure Adisa's spear tasted more Orcovan blood before the ordeal was finished.

Finnian had been fighting next to Kieran, and he was genuinely impressed with his performance. He obviously had little experience, his technique was occasionally sloppy, and his timing needed some work, but Kieran was showing a lot of promise as a fighter. With more training and experience, Kieran could be a great swordsman.

Kieran's mind was racing a mile per minute. It was so easy to throw caution into the wind and fight with raw emotion, but he constantly reminded himself that that was precisely what could get you killed. If you fight with pure emotion, you get haphazard and impulsive. He had to remember his training and study his opponents, analyze their every move.

Every now and then Kieran would catch a glimpse of Finnian in the corner of his eye, and even though Finnian was busy with his own opponents, it gave him a sense of security knowing that one of the finest swordsmen in Hume was nearby.

Finnian saw Aidan from afar. He turned to Kieran and called out his name. He turned toward Finnian and waited for instruction. Finnian pointed off in the distance, and Kieran's eyes followed the trajectory. He saw Aidan and Connor and understood the message. Finnian wanted him to start making his way toward them.

Kieran nodded in reply, and the two started to make their way toward their king. Aidan was an experienced fighter, but he was also older than most soldiers in the Human army. Finnian would feel more comfortable if he stayed close to Aidan.

The battle continued to rage throughout the morning. The Serpens and the Union soldiers were taking heavy casualties, but the situation was more desperate for the Orcovans. More than half of the Orcs had already been killed or wounded, and the tide of the battle was showing no signs of turning.

Aidan surveyed the battlefield and hailed Connor. Connor quickly rode over to him.

After Connor arrived, Aidan said, "Try to regroup one battalion soldiers in front of the city and guard that breach in the wall. I'm sure our soldiers protecting the city can handle them, but I don't want to take any chances."

Connor nodded and said, "Yes, my king." He rode off and began giving orders to the officers.

Unfortunately, the order came too late. A small group of Orcs broke through the line and made a push toward the broken wall. The nearby Union soldiers realized what was happening and raced the advancing Orcs to the wall.

The Orcs won the race. They ran through the wall and were met with some resistance, but unfortunately, most of the soldiers that were stationed within the city had filed out onto the battlefield to join the action. The Orcs easily overcame the few soldiers who did stay behind and began entering the nearby buildings searching for civilians. Thankfully, they found none because everyone was still safely housed within the underground bunkers.

The Union soldiers followed shortly behind them, and because it was only a small group, they were able to eliminate these invaders one by one. What could have been a disaster had been averted.

The soldiers resolved to stay close to the wall for the remainder of the fight to keep the same thing from happening a second time.

It was now after noon, and the number of Orcovan warriors still fit for battle were only a quarter of what they were at the start, but the progress of the battle had slowed some. The Orcs had huddled together in formation, creating a shield wall around them with their archers firing on their enemies. Their archers were the only effective part of their tactics, but their arrow supply was beginning to run low.

The Serpens employed the same tactics they did during the initial charge at the beginning of the battle, but they, too, were running low on arrows. Even so, their speed and spear strikes on the shield wall continued to chip away at the Orcovan numbers. Any stragglers that had been isolated from the group fought ferociously, but they couldn't last long when isolated from the rest of their fellow Orcs.

Finnian, Kieran, Aidan, Connor, and a platoon of other Human soldiers were locked in a vicious fight with a group of Orcs that had been cut off from the main group.

Finnian and Connor each picked up spears off the ground and hurled them at the Orcs, forcing them to bring up their shields. When they did, both of the men rushed in. Finnian got checked by an Orc shield and was thrown straight back onto the ground. It was a sobering reminder of how much stronger they were than Humans.

He shuffled to get back onto his feet, for he knew that the Orc would be rushing him when he realized he had knocked him down. He looked and, sure enough, he saw the Orc rushing at him with his sword cocked back, ready to be thrust down toward Finnian.

He tried his hardest to get off the ground in time, but he knew that the Orc would reach him before he could. He waited for the Orc to get close, and when he did, Finnian swung his sword using both hands and batted the Orc's sword to the side as he thrust it downward. The Orc's sword stabbed into the ground only inches from Finnian's head.

Finnian swiftly and smoothly drew his dagger with his right hand and shoved it directly into the eye slit of the Orc's faceplate. Blood poured out onto Finnian's face as the large, heavy body of the Orc fell on top of him. Finnian mustered his strength and rolled the limp body off him just in time to see a second Orc rushing forward. Finnian watched him advance as he tried to reposition his sword to defend himself.

Just as the Orc was within thrusting range, a spear glanced off the chest plate of the Orc and he paused to look for the source of the thrown spear.

Aidan had picked up a spear and hurled it at the last second, then sprinted forward. He collided with the Orc soon after the spear had landed, and Aidan's well-positioned sword stabbed into the Orc's chest through the opening in his armor in the left armpit.

The Orc was alive but injured. Aidan withdrew his sword and swung it horizontally across the Orc's neck, and blood spurted from the wound. The Orc frantically grabbed at his neck and stumbled backward onto the ground, bleeding out.

Aidan looked down at Finnian extending his hand, and he grabbed it and stood up. He stared at Aidan and was about to thank him, but Aidan simply patted him on the shoulder and turned to keep fighting.

Finnian already had too many close calls. Sooner or later, his luck would run out and a friend wouldn't be nearby to rescue him. He had killed a lot of Orcs in this fight, but he needed to slow down and keep his head clear.

"Don't fight with emotion. Fight with patience, with clarity," Finnian told himself.

This segregated group of Orcs they had been fighting was declining in numbers, but the fight was nonetheless still a struggle. The Orcs were surrounded by Serpen and Union forces and knew that this would only end one way for them, but they were committed to fight to the very last warrior standing. One couldn't help admire their resolve even in the face of certain death.

Aidan and Connor did their best to keep their distance from the action and direct their soldiers, but there were no longer any discernable battles lines. The field was a massive brawl.

Aidan watched as a group of Humans and Dwarves engaged a huddled squad of Orcs. He saw an intact spear lying on the ground and decided he would lend a hand. He bent over, grasped the spear, and as he stood back up, he was struck in the chest by an Orcovan arrow.

He dropped the spear and stumbled into a seated position on the ground, gasping for air. The arrow had penetrated through the chest plate of his armor and pierced his left lung. Aidan struggled to take deep breaths, but every time he tried, he would cough bright red blood.

Finnian looked over his shoulder to where Aidan had been standing several seconds prior, and he saw him sitting on the ground with an arrow protruding from his chest.

Finnian screamed, *"Aidan!"* and sprinted toward him.

When he reached him, he knelt, took off his helm, then removed Aidan's. Aidan had a small amount of blood running down his chin as he continued to gasp for air. Every breath he drew was accompanied by a wheezing and rattling sound. Finnian had heard that sound before. The wound was deep into Aidan's lung.

Tears began to fill Finnian's eyes. He struggled to speak. "Aidan . . . No . . . Deep breaths! Keep breathing!" Tears were streaming down Finnian's face.

Aidan reached up and rested his hand on Finnian's cheek. The two looked at one another, neither of them speaking. Aidan gave a slight smile as he looked upon Finnian's face, the face of the boy he loved like a second son, one . . . last . . . time.

His vision slowly faded to black, and his hand fell to his side. Aidan was gone.

Finnian felt utterly broken. He had lost the man whom he looked up to the most. He had lost . . . another father.

Tears continued to pour down his face as he gently rested Aidan's head on the ground.

By now, the soldiers had finished off the remainder of the segregated group of Orcs, and they all rushed to Finnian's side and stared in disbelief as they looked upon Aidan's body lying on the ground.

Kieran stood in silence as he watched his captain cry over the body of his king. He could hardly take the whole scene in. He had a multitude of emotions welling up inside of him. He was heartbroken. He was angry. He was confused. Kieran had had his first real taste of war, and he was already exhausted of it. He now had only one overwhelming desire: He wanted to go home.

Connor wiped tears from his eyes and knelt and rested his hand on Finnian's shoulder, and the two knelt beside Aidan's body for a long time without speaking.

~

Shortly after Aidan's death, the remaining Orcs sounded their battle horns to signal a retreat. The battle was won. The remaining Serpens and Union soldiers roared triumphantly, and there was celebration all across the battlefield. Had they known of Aidan's death at the time, no one would have celebrated.

Finnian composed himself, stood up, and looked out over the field. There was one thing left for him to do: He had to find Reagan.

The soldiers quickly went into the bunkers and proclaimed their victory to the people, and they began filing out. Some celebrated, but most were reserved any celebration until they could ensure their sons, husbands, or fathers had survived the battle. Tragically, many would be not be celebrating.

Finnian entered the city through the gate and began filtering through the crowds, looking for Reagan. The city streets were filled with masses of people searching for their loved ones, but Finnian knew that the royal family would make their way toward the palace so they would be easier to find. He made his way through the crowded streets and finally arrived at the stairwell leading up to the palace.

He saw her standing at the foot of the steps, auburn hair glowing in the afternoon sun. She, Evelyn, and Owen were together, searching through the crowds for any sight of Aidan and Finnian. Though Finnian was barely composing himself over Aidan's death, the sight of Reagan brought him renewed strength. She was unharmed!

Finnian ran toward her. She spotted him and called out, "Finnian!" and ran toward him. The two embraced one another in the midst of the crowd, Reagan crying tears of joy onto Finnian's armor. Hugging a man in a suit of armor was quite uncomfortable, but she didn't care in the slightest. Neither of them spoke, nor did they need to speak.

Somehow, their embrace communicated more than words could express at that moment.

Evelyn and Owen caught up with them and they, too, hugged Finnian. Evelyn, also crying tears of joy, said, "I can't tell you how much grief the news of your disappearance caused us. It's so good to have you back! Whether you realize it or not, you're a part of this family, Finnian!"

Reagan wiped the tears from her eye and finally said, "Where's my father?"

All of Finnian's renewed vigor instantly melted away, and tears began to fill his eyes. He glanced down at the ground, then back up at Evelyn.

It was all the answer they needed. Evelyn stumbled down into a seated position on the ground, hands covering her face as she sobbed. Owen knelt and wrapped his arms around her, trying to comfort her. Tears began to stream heavily down Reagan's face as she embraced Finnian once more. There the four remained, consoling one another for a long time as the crowds scurried around them.

~

The news of Aidan's death began to spread throughout the city, as well as among the soldiers. What was once a time of celebration quickly became a time of mourning. Aidan was a beloved king to all of Hume, and his loss was met with anger and denial by the people.

Connor, Oleg, Amrynn, and Finnian retrieved Aidan's body from the battlefield. They removed the arrow, covered the body with a red silk cloth, and slowly and respectfully began carrying it into the city toward the palace. The surviving Elves, Dwarves, and even the Serpens stood in silence as they carried Aidan's body through the city gates.

As they traveled through the streets of Hume, the soldiers removed their helms, the people removed their hats, and all were silent. There was not a dry eye in the crowd as all began to kneel and bow their heads when Aidan's body passed by them.

Finnian, Connor, Oleg, and Amrynn each had tears in their eyes as they approached the palace steps where the royal family waited. Evelyn, Owen, and Reagan watched and cried as Aidan was brought home for the final time.

~

The Serpens collected their dead and bid Connor, Oleg, and Amrynn farewell. Davu, their second in command behind Adisa, offered his deepest condolences for the death of Aidan, and he even claimed that he would gladly trade places with him if it meant Hume could have her king back.

Their losses during the Battle of Enlanor had been substantial, with at least one-third of their forces killed, including their high commander, Adisa.

Upon hearing the news of Adisa's death, Connor began to apologize, but Davu held up his hand and said, "Stop. It is for this very purpose that we Serpen warriors were bred. We live so that we may have the privilege of serving our king, Zesiro. Our brother Adisa has faithfully completed his mission in the service of his king." Davu paused for a moment, then added, "We Serpens have an old proverb that has been passed down over the generations: 'The pain of separation never overcomes the joy of remembrance.' Our brother Adisa will be missed, but the time we had by his side will be celebrated. His work is now finished, and he can rest."

Connor, Oleg, and Amrynn didn't know how to respond. They were at a loss for words. The Serpens had a sense of honor a sacrifice that no one would have ever expected. To consider one's own life as an offering to be poured out in the service of another required a level of humility that is alien to most people.

Davu bowed in a farewell, and the Serpens began their travel home. As mysteriously as they had arrived in Hume, they were gone.

~

Finnian joined the royal family in the palace. He found them all in the great hall, sitting at a table. Owen and Reagan were comforting Evelyn, who had waited for the privacy of the palace to let her emotions pour out. Her face was buried in her arms as she openly cried. Reagan and Owen hugged her from each side, but no one spoke. There was nothing either of them could say at this moment, but they could be there for her.

Finnian sat down at the table next to Reagan, and Evelyn lifted her head and looked at him. She reached her hand out and rested it on his and asked, "Were you there when it happened?"

Finnian bowed his head and, fighting back tears, gently nodded.

"Did he say anything?" she replied.

Finnian's mind recalled the moment of Aidan's death, and he couldn't hold the tears back any longer. A single drop cascaded down his left cheek.

He finally shook his head and said, "No. He only looked at me and smiled. He was at peace."

Evelyn mustered the best smile she could and said, "I'm glad you were with him at the end." She dabbed her runny nose with a handkerchief and stood up from the table, saying, "Forgive me, but I am going to retire to our . . . *my* bedroom. I need to be alone." Finnian, Reagan, and Owen watched her stand and walk out of the great hall.

Owen had been handling the situation with stoicism. He knew he needed to be strong for the sake of his family and for Hume.

Owen turned to the others and said, "I think I'm going to retire as well." He leaned over, hugged Reagan, then Finnian, and left the great hall.

Reagan rested her head on Finnian's shoulder. There they sat with one another for a while longer. Though their reunion wasn't as joyous as each of them had expected it would be, they were both thankful to have each other at a time such as this. Reagan eventually announced that she too would retire, and she kissed Finnian on the cheek and bid him a good night.

Finnian returned to the barracks and stayed in his bunk the rest of the evening. The events of the battle kept replaying in his mind. Twice he should have been killed, but each time, a savior showed up just the right time. What are the chances? Why did he survive when Aidan did not?

Finnian's mind drifted to Kieran. There was no way he was going to be able to sleep anytime soon, so he decided to get out of his bunk and find him.

It didn't take long for Finnian to find him. Kieran had been lying in his bunk writing a letter to his family to let them know he was alive. They would undoubtedly be worried about him when the news of the battle reached his hometown of Cliften.

He saw Finnian approaching, and he rose to his feet and said, "Good evening, Captain."

Finnian gave him a slight nod and replied, "How are you feeling?"

Kieran paused for a moment, then said, "As well as I can, I suppose." Kieran studied Finnian's face and continued, "What about you, Captain?"

Finnian cracked a slight smile and replied, "As well as I can, I suppose." He took a deep breath and let it out. "Listen, I wanted to thank you for what you did out on the battlefield today." He paused for a moment, then concluded, "You saved my life."

Kieran shook his head. "I was just in the right place at the right time."

"Even so, you did very well out there. I was watching you, and you have good instincts. You're going to be a very fine soldier," said Finnian.

Kieran remained silent for an instant, then said, "I have three years left of my mandated service. After that, I'm hanging up my sword."

One week ago, Finnian would have rebuked him for letting his ability go to waste. Instead, Finnian simply nodded and asked, "Do you have a girl back home?"

Kieran shook his head.

"What about that cute brunette I saw working at your family's pub?" replied Finnian.

Kieran laughed, saying, "You mean my sister?"

Finnian grimaced. "That's probably not going to work . . ."

They both laughed and were thankful for some comic relief on a day that had been plagued by tragedy. They continued talking for another hour, discussing their hometowns, their families, and their experiences in the Human army. They had each recently lost a dear friend. Kieran had lost Donal, and Finnian had lost Galen. This was the first time either of them really had a chance to talk about it, and in some way, they each were able to obtain a sense of closure by sharing one another's burden. At the end of the hour, Finnian started to get tired and left Kieran to his letter writing so he could get some rest.

~

Aidan's funeral was held the following day. Members of the royal family in Hume were laid to rest in the Grave of Kings, a cemetery adjacent to the palace within the city walls.

The public funeral was held at the steps to the palace, and all in Enlanor who were able to attend were present. Aidan's body was placed in a beautiful ceremonial casket identical to the ones used by every king before him, and it was displayed at the foot of the palace steps.

Commander Connor officiated the public service. He recounted the king's life, military career, and accomplishments, all of which is the formality of such events. Connor thought it shallow, impersonal, and an affront to one of the greatest men he had ever known. However, this was the tradition, and he was the highest-ranking official in Hume for the time being. The responsibility was his to bear.

The personal funeral was something different entirely. After Connor was finished, he, Owen, Oleg, Amrynn, and Finnian carried the casket up the steps to the royal cemetery while the family and close friends of the king followed. Connor led the casket in the front while the remaining four carried it with two on each side. Every other person present bowed before the king one final time as his casket was carried away.

The casket was rested on the ground near the sepulcher, and the mourners stood around it. The private funeral was a time for those close to the deceased to each have an opportunity to give a brief eulogy in remembrance of their lost loved one. Those present were the remainder of the royal family, Finnian, Connor, Oleg, and Amrynn.

Connor stepped forward and spoke first. "Many kings have come and gone throughout Hume's history. I am too young to have known any others, but I do know one thing: You were the most honorable and noblest man I've ever known, and I am honored to have served under you. You were a great leader and an even greater friend. Good-bye, my king." Connor kneeled before the casket and stepped back.

King Amrynn stepped forward next. "I *am* old enough to have known your father, King Nolan. He was a beloved and honorable king, and you would have made him proud. I've told you many times that you reminded me of your father, and it was always because you shared those same great qualities." Amrynn turned to the royal family and said, "I count myself fortunate to have known Aidan, and I offer you my deepest condolences." He turned toward the casket and finished with, "Fare thee well, my friend." Amrynn bowed and stepped back.

King Oleg stepped forward. He was never much for words, and when he did speak, he was certainly not very eloquent or articulate. Nobody expected much from him now. However, Oleg stood before the casket and surprised everyone by saying, "Hume mourns the loss of its king today, but like the others here by my side, I mourn for the loss of more than a king. I mourn for the loss of a friend. Your wisdom, respect, and hospitality were a welcome addition to the council, and you somehow managed to even out my brash stubbornness and quick temper." There were a couple of small laughs from the other council members. Oleg continued, "Someone wiser than myself recently told me that the 'pain of separation never overcomes the joy of remembrance.' How true that is, old friend. You will be greatly missed, but I will always remember our time together with fondness and gratitude. Good-bye, my friend." He kneeled before the casket and stepped back.

Owen surprisingly stepped forward next. No one had expected him to speak at all. He began, "I may be young and have little life experience, but one thing I do know is that I couldn't have asked for a better man than you to be my father." Owen paused, fighting back tears and the catch in his throat. He finally continued, "I don't know how I could ever fill your shoes, but I will do my best to make you proud. I love you, Father." Owen kneeled before the casket and stepped back.

Finnian stepped forward, bowing his head. He remained silent for several moments, then began, "I lost my father when I was eight years old. I lost my mother six years later. By the time I first met you five years ago, I had forgotten what it felt like to have a family, but you welcomed me into yours as if I was one of your own. You counseled me, you supported me . . . You helped me realize what it's like to have a family again. I have lost not one, but *two* fathers." Finnian took a deep breath and exhaled slowly. "Good-bye . . . Father."

Evelyn and Reagan stayed silent. There was much they wanted to say, but neither had the strength to offer any more words. The group stood in silence for some time, and then the men quietly walked up to the casket and carried it into the sepulcher. They carefully set it down next to King Nolan's casket, Aidan's father. They all bowed one last time, then exited and locked the doors. Aidan had joined the kings of Hume in his final resting place.

15

IT WAS ONE week after Aidan's funeral, and the seventeen-year-old Prince Owen was to be officially crowned king of Hume. The ceremony was set to take place at noon, and the royal family was in the midst of preparing.

Finnian had stayed in a spare bedroom of the palace since Aidan's funeral. Evelyn offered for him to stay, and Connor granted him a temporary leave on the grounds that he was mourning the loss of a family member, which from a certain perspective, was true. Finnian was dressed in a decorative suit of ceremonial armor, the only appropriate dress attire for a soldier.

Evelyn and Reagan wore fine silk dresses, both of which were green. Green was the official color worn by royalty in Hume. Each of them wore their crowns signifying their titles as queen and princess.

Owen wore his finest surcoat and cloak, also green in color. He wore his golden crown signifying his title as prince of Hume, which he would soon be retiring.

Owen was waiting in the great hall, dressed and ready for the ceremony. Evelyn and Reagan met him and both commented on how handsome he looked and gave him words of encouragement. Finnian joined them shortly after and offered the same encouragements.

Owen turned to them with a pale look on his face and said, "I'm not ready for this. I'm not even old enough to fight yet, and now I'm going to be king of Hume?" He sighed and looked at the ground while shaking his head. "I have no idea what I'm doing."

Evelyn walked up to Owen and hugged him. She looked at him and said, "Have I ever told you about the day your father was crowned king?"

Owen shook his head.

Evelyn continued, "He wasn't that much older than you . . . about Finnian's age. His father had just died, and it was time for him to assume the throne, just like you. He and I stood in this very hall, and do you know what he said to me?"

Owen stared at his mother blankly.

"He said the exact same thing you just said. He told me he wasn't ready for a responsibility like this, and he was terrified he would make some huge mistake that would cause Hume to go to ruin." Evelyn laughed, then continued, "It's remarkable how similar you two are. I see the same qualities in you that made your father a great king. I know you don't feel ready, but trust me, you are going to be a great king . . . just like him."

Owen's eyes began to fill with tears. "I miss him so much . . ." he said as he sniffed.

Evelyn hugged Owen again and said, "So do we, dear . . . but you will carry on his legacy. And in that way, he will live on . . . through you."

Owen dabbed each eye with a sleeve of his surcoat, nodded, stood up straight. "Well, I suppose we shouldn't keep Hume waiting."

~

Owen's coronation was conducted in front of the palace steps, the same place as Aidan's funeral a week before. Thousands upon thousands were in attendance. Kings Amrynn and Oleg stayed in Hume for the coronation, and their families traveled from their provinces to be present as well.

Still being the highest-ranking official in Hume, Connor officiated the ceremony. When the time for the crowning had come, Owen kneeled before Evelyn, and she placed Aidan's crown on his head. Owen rose, and at that moment, he was no longer a prince. He was now Owen, son of Aidan, king of Hume, 1127 of the Fourth Age.

The crowd roared their applause, and King Owen stood before the masses feeling a mixture of terror and excitement. He discreetly nodded and whispered to himself, "I can do this." He was his father's son, and if he was even half the man his father was, he would lead the province of Hume well.

Finnian looked upon his new king, Owen. He had known Owen since he was a young boy of thirteen, and he had grown into a very fine young man. Finnian thought that he barely even recognized Owen at that moment. He appeared more kingly and noble than ever before, and Finnian had the utmost confidence that he would be a great king, just like his father. Finnian loved Owen like a brother, and he beamed with pride.

~

Finnian and the royal family returned to the palace after the coronation had ended, and Evelyn suggested they have a big feast for dinner to celebrate as a family, just as she and Aidan had done when he was crowned king so many years ago.

For the first time since Aidan's death, things almost seemed normal again. The family talked and laughed all throughout the meal, and Reagan even teased Owen about how she was confident that her younger brother would run Hume right into the ground.

All seemed in good spirits except Finnian. Throughout the dinner, he seemed distant and bothered by something. At one point, Reagan leaned over and whispered into his ear, "Are you all right?"

Finnian smiled at her and nodded. Though it did not seem like it to her, it was indeed the truth. Finnian was more all right now than he had been in a long time. Even though the man he looked up to the most was gone, he finally had clarity and was at peace.

He loved being a soldier and he loved serving Hume, but there was something he loved more—the princess of Hume. He had spent his whole adult life fighting the Orcs thinking he would finally appease his resentment and pain, but as Aidan had once told him years ago, revenge is a fool's game. He had longed to heal from his lost childhood family by fighting the ones who took them away, and he ignored the new family he had had for the past five years.

His closest friend, Galen, had often talked about wanting to retire from active service in the Human army, find a nice girl, settle down, and start a family. At the time, Finnian had laughed at him. He told him he'd have plenty of time for that after his prime fighting years had left him, but now Galen would never get the chance. Finnian had watched his closest friend die in the forest. It took him being captured, being carted to Serpenta, and facing his own mortality to finally wake up and realize just how foolish he had been.

Aidan was gone, taken by the very same hands as his parents. But for the first time in his life, he didn't think about revenge. He didn't have the lust for battle. He simply mourned for not spending more time with Aidan, and he wanted to not waste any more opportunities to be with his new family. He knew what he must do. Finnian looked at Owen and thought, *But, there's one thing I must do first . . .*

~

After the dinner had ended, the four of them decided to go to the palace library for drinks and dessert. They sat together at a table and shared their favorite stories about Aidan for the next couple of hours.

Reagan and Evelyn eventually announced that they were exhausted and must go to bed. They wished Owen and Finnian a good night, and left for their bedrooms upstairs.

Owen turned to Finnian and said, "It's been a long day for me, so I think I'll turn in for the night as well."

Finnian smiled and replied, "Of course, but if it is not too much of an inconvenience, there is something I'd like to discuss with you first."

"Yes?" said Owen. He wasn't sure what to expect, but Finnian had seemed off the entire night. He figured something must have been bothering him.

Finnian got out of his chair and knelt before Owen and said, "Owen, son of Aidan, you are my king. And I, Captain Finnian, must ask for my king's permission to marry the princess of Hume."

Owen's face lit up and he filled the library with laughter as he replied, "Get up, Finnian! You have my mother's blessing, I knew my

CAMERON COWBURN

father well enough to know that you had his blessing, and you, *of course*, have my blessing! You're already like an older brother to me, Finnian. If you would have waited any longer, I suspect that, as your king, I would have *ordered* you to marry her!"

Finnian stood up, and the two laughed and hugged each other. After ending the hug, Owen shrugged and said, "Well? What are you waiting for?"

Finnian smiled, nodded, and jogged out of the library, toward the staircase leading to the upstairs bedrooms.

Owen followed Finnian out, and they walked up the stairs together. When at the top, Finnian turned left toward Reagan's bedroom, and Owen turned right toward Evelyn's.

Owen knocked on Evelyn's door. She opened the door and said, "What is it, Owen?"

Owen smiled and said, "Come take a walk down the hallway with me."

"Now?" Evelyn replied.

"Yes. Trust me," he answered.

The two walked down the hall toward Reagan's bedroom, and they stopped at a point where they could see Finnian at Reagan's door but not close enough so as to intrude.

Evelyn turned to Owen, and with an enormous smile, he said, "He just asked for my permission to marry Reagan."

Evelyn gasped with excitement. She said, "We won't be able to hear them! We need to get closer!"

Owen rolled his eyes. "It's going to be awkward enough with us standing here watching them! We don't need to be closer."

"Ugh . . . Fine . . .," replied Evelyn.

Finnian stood at Reagan's door. He took a deep breath and tried to calm his heart rate. He thought to himself, *I've been in combat numerous times. Why am I so nervous?* He raised his hand and knocked on Reagan's door.

Reagan came to the door, and when she saw him standing there, she said, "Finnian? Is something wrong?"

Finnian smiled and nodded. "Yes, something is wrong." He took another deep breath and continued, "I must ask for your forgiveness. My parents were killed by Orcs when I was a boy, and my entire life has revolved around honing my skills in battle to vent my anger and get revenge. I let my pain and emotions drive me, and I failed to see the blessings in my life that have been right in front of me for years. It took me getting captured, hauled away to a foreign land, and thinking I was knocking on death's door to finally wake up and see just what I've been neglecting. When I was in that Serpentan cell, the only thing I wanted to do was see your face one more time. I love you, Reagan, and I've been a fool."

Finnian took Reagan by the hand and knelt before her. "I, Finnian, ask the princess of Hume for forgiveness, and if she will have me, I ask for her hand in marriage."

Reagan was utterly speechless, and tears of joy began running down her face. She finally managed to say, "The princess of Hume accepts!"

The two of them smiled and embraced one other, and Evelyn and Owen quickly rushed over and joined the betrothed couple.

Reagan laughed and said, "It sure took you long enough! Don't expect me accept procrastination like that when we're married!"

"I'll try to work on it!" replied Finnian as he laughed along with her.

~

The marriage was scheduled for two days later. Both Finnian and Reagan would have preferred to have a small, simple ceremony; however, that was not exactly an option for a royal wedding.

Typically, a royal wedding would be scheduled further out than two days, but the royal families from Elvenna and Dwarvonia were already in Hume for Owen's coronation. Amrynn and Oleg very much wanted to be present for the wedding, so it was decided to have the ceremony while they and their families were still in the city.

The wedding was held again on the palace steps. This location was favored for high-profile events due to its ease of accessibility to the citizens of Hume.

CAMERON COWBURN

Most of the city's population attended, which made Finnian very uncomfortable. He was a simple soldier and was not much used to this level of attention. However, he knew that he would have no choice from here on out, for his marriage to Reagan would make him a prince of Hume.

It was customary for any royal wedding to be officiated by the king himself, and Owen had actually vomited out of nervousness earlier in the morning. He had only been king for three days, and he in no way felt ready to officiate a royal wedding.

Evelyn had spent the last two days coaching him and giving him notes, but he was still nonetheless nervous. Thankfully, not much speaking was necessary during a wedding in Hume. Evelyn had teased Owen that he should be fortunate he was not the king of Elvenna, for Elven weddings typically lasted at least three hours.

The ceremony began with Owen proceeding down the steps of the palace entrance and welcoming the crowd. He would have to project his voice as much as he could, but obviously there would be many attending that wouldn't be able to hear the ceremony.

When Owen reached the bottom of the steps, he announced, "Friends, the king of Hume would like to personally welcome you all to this joyous occasion! I have the privilege of officiating the ceremony of marriage between my beloved sister, Princess Reagan, and Captain Finnian of the Human army. I would like to call them forward now."

The attention of the audience turned to the top of the palace stairs. Finnian and Reagan appeared and began to descend the stairs in their wedding attire. They were in fact wearing the exact same clothing as they did during Owen's coronation.

Finnian was clad in a fine suit of armor, save for the helm. His dark brown hair was neatly combed and hung down to roughly four inches above each shoulder, and he had a single thin braid that ran down the left side of his face. His armor had been polished to a perfect shine, something he desperately struggled to keep clean for the entire morning.

Reagan wore a beautiful green silk dress. Her auburn hair flowed freely down over her shoulders, and she had several braids with small white flowers intertwined in them.

The large crowd cheered and applauded as the couple descended the stairs. When they reached the bottom, they stood in front of Owen, facing one another and holding hands. Owen gave a summary of Finnian's history, including his hometown, his parents, and the highlights of his military career. He then did the same with Reagan, mentioning that she was born and raised in Enlanor and was raised by Aidan and Evelyn, though this was merely a formality. Every citizen of Hume was obviously familiar with the princess of Hume.

While Owen spoke, Reagan and Finnian stared into one another's eyes, both smiling from ear to ear. Finnian couldn't help but think about how beautiful Reagan looked at that moment and wondered why he had put this off for so long.

After finishing with the backgrounds of each, Owen continued, "Captain Finnian and Princess Reagan announced their intention to be husband and wife just two days ago, and I could not be more pleased. I have had the privilege of knowing Captain Finnian for the past five years. I love him like my own brother, and I wholeheartedly welcome him into the royal family of Hume as its newest prince. And so, before the citizens of Andruvia, I hereby declare that they are now joined as husband and wife until death parts them!"

Finnian and Reagan shared a kiss, and the city roared its approval. The sound was nearly deafening! The newlyweds then faced the crowd and raised their clasped hands high, signifying they were now officially joined together as husband and wife.

Owen leaned in and said to Finnian, "Just because you are officially my older brother now doesn't mean you can give me orders!"

Finnian laughed and replied, "Well, maybe I should check the records of the law just to be sure!"

Owen laughed and said, "You have to be able to read to do that!"

Both Finnian and Reagan joined him in laughter, and Owen leaned back out. As most weddings did, the celebration lasted for the remainder of the evening, though this particular celebration was city-wide.

~

CAMERON COWBURN

Finnian's official coronation was performed by Owen four days later. Before the whole city, he knelt before Owen, and he placed his previous crown upon Finnian's head. Finnian considered it an honor to bear the old crown of the young man he could now proudly call his brother.

During the coronation, Finnian couldn't help but recollect the events over the past few weeks and marvel at how much things had changed. He had gone from being the orphaned boy who was serving as a captain in the army to being the happily married prince of Hume with a new family that he adored. The course of the royal family's lives, the Andruvian Union, Orcova, and even the mysterious province of Serpenta had changed with one solitary act by Aquaria, the most modest of the provinces, and brought Andruvia into a new era—the Fifth Age.

EPILOGUE

*I*T'S A TAD *cold tonight*, thought Finnian as he stepped outside his office. He had finished reviewing the patrol reports for the day, and he had stepped outside for some fresh air and to smoke from his pipe as he read the letter from Kieran that he had just received.

He opened up the letter and read:

Finnian,

Things are going well! Business at the Yellow Oak is as good as ever, and Fiona and I are excited for our wedding next month. You better be here for that! I can't have my closest friend skip my own wedding! In fact, you better come and visit before then! I'm too busy running my family's business to travel, and I know how little work you officers do, so the burden is on you! I'll keep a fresh mug ready for you.

Kieran

Finnian finished reading the letter and laughed as he slid it into his pocket. It was time to return home to the palace for the night. He drew a deep breath and felt thankful for the chance to stretch his legs after having sat behind his desk all afternoon.

It was a beautiful, cool evening, and the sun was just beginning to set below the horizon. He looked at the sky and admired the streaks of yellow and orange from the evening's sunset.

~

Five years had passed since the Battle of Enlanor. Prince Finnian was promoted to the rank of major, overseeing the Northern Hume patrol. His duties rarely required him to leave Enlanor, which was the way he liked it. It allowed him to return to the palace and be with his wife and four-year-old son every night.

Hume had seen the smallest amount of Orcovan activity within the country since the start of the Fourth Age. After being defeated in the Battle of Enlanor, raiding parties were rarely ever seen in Northern Hume, though everyone suspected they would one day return. War was a significant part of Orcovan culture, and the patrols in Hume made it a priority to remain vigilant.

The Serpens had wasted no time in attacking Aquaria after the meeting in Dunsbury. The Aquarians were completely caught off guard by the invasion, and they were no match for the military might of Serpenta. The Aquarian capital of Manoi was destroyed, and the Aquarian King Dalip was captured and personally executed by King Zesiro himself.

Since then, the relations between Aquaria and Hume were actually the best they had ever been. Their new king, Famas, had pushed for reconciliation with the Humans after having witnessed firsthand the consequences of their hatred and scheming. The leaders of the Andruvian Union were understandably very reluctant to offer Aquaria admittance into the Union, but the topic had been repeatedly discussed for the past year now.

Zesiro and his queen, Arjana, had another litter of children shortly after the destruction of Manoi. They named the firstborn male of the litter Jabari, prince of Serpenta, royal heir to the throne.

The leaders of the Andruvian Union extended an invitation to Zesiro to join the Union, but the offer was declined. The Serpens are and will always be a proud and self-sufficient nation, with little interest in maintaining foreign relations.

King Owen was proving to be a great king like his father, Aidan. He had developed a strong rapport with Commander Connor, and his approval among the citizens of Hume was even greater than that of his father.

As king, Owen was exempt from having to serve in the Human army, but he insisted to undergo military training almost every day. He fully expected to accompany his soldiers on the battlefield should the need arise, though Connor had tried to dissuade him many times. The personality of Owen was so similar to his father's that Connor often felt as though Aidan had never actually left.

A monument to the Battle of Enlanor was erected in Hume, honoring those who fought and died defending the city. It had been the largest battle Hume had seen in the Fourth Age, and Owen had ordered the monument's construction in the months following his coronation. The monument consisted of four bronze statues of a Human, an Elf, a Dwarf, and a Serpen standing side by side in full battle dress. Underneath them was a plaque that read:

Dedicated to those who fought and died in the
Battle of Enlanor, 1127, Fourth Age

and in remembrance of

King Aidan of Hume, son of King Nolan
1080–1127, Fourth Age

~

Finnian began walking toward the palace and stopped at the monument, taking time to admire it. After several minutes, he slowly ran his fingertips across Aidan's name on the plaque, then continued his walk toward the palace.

He walked up the palace stairs and into its entrance. He found Reagan in the courtyard watching their son as he chased a butterfly around the courtyard. He walked up behind her, wrapped his arms around her, and rested his head on her shoulder. His arms cradled Reagan's distended pregnant belly.

She smiled and said, "How was the day?"

"Good. Quiet," replied Finnian. "I got a letter from Kieran today, and he's already insisting that we come and visit him again."

Reagan smiled while rolling her eyes. "We were just there two weeks ago! He just needs to move to the city!"

Finnian nodded. "I know . . . I keep telling him that, but he's loving running his family's pub. I don't see it happening."

"Well, we can still keep pestering him, anyway," said Reagan.

"Oh, I certainly will!" replied Finnian.

He spun Reagan around so they were facing one another and gave her a small kiss.

"How are you feeling?" he asked.

"Not terrible. My lower back still hurts, but nothing out of the ordinary," she said.

Finnian motioned toward their son and asked, "How was he today?"

Reagan laughed and replied, "Oh, the usual. I can barely keep this boy inside long enough to eat. All he wants is to be outside." She called out to the boy, "Aidan, look who's home!"

Aidan turned and saw his mother and father standing together in the courtyard. He gave a huge smile and let out a small screech and ran toward them as quickly as his little legs could carry him. Finnian bent down with wide arms and scooped Aidan off the ground, hugging him tightly as he spun him around.

Finnian looked at Aidan and said, "Why don't we go inside and have something to eat?"

The little boy laughed and nodded.

The three of them walked toward the courtyard exit just as the last remnants of the sun sank below the horizon.